T0064068

3D DREAMS
DESIRES
DESTINY

3D DREAMS DESIRES DESTINY

DEEKSHA PANDEY

PARTRIDGE
A Penguin Random House Company

ISBN: Hardcover   978-1-4828-5059-8
            Softcover   978-1-4828-5058-1
            eBook   978-1-4828-5057-4

Print information available on the last page.

To order additional copies of this book, contact
Partridge India
000 800 10062 62
orders.india@partridgepublishing.com

www.partridgepublishing.com/india

To

KRISH

Who taught me,

'Every story should have a Moral'

Contents

Part II

Acknowledgement

Vivek, this work matured till completion
only because of your support;

You helped me regain the strength
whenever I was about to abort.

Mom, Dad, and those for me who are
much more than Mom, Dad,

This is a surprise gift for you four; hope it makes you glad.

Bro and sis, your encouragement is treasured;

Affection or appreciation, whatever it
was, it's difficult to be measured.

Binita, Rishi Sir, Amritha, your adorations,
suggestions meant a lot;

Before you read it, to me it looked
like a dubious blind spot.

Thanks to Farina, Joe, and Marie for
giving my dream a shape;

With your help, my thoughts could
get this impressive drape.

Hope the message reaches where I want it to go.

Let all boys and girls imbibe it; the
teaching should retain its flow.

Thanks to all those who gave me the
story, the courage, and the passion.

Let disseminating awareness become the
new trend in literary fashion.

Prologue

'Life is a ticket to the biggest drama on earth.' Amazing!

Ten words so aptly put together to reveal the biggest mystery, which is *life*. In front of Mahim Church, Mumbai, I sat in an Innova and was on my way to Chhatrapati Shivaji International Airport. Life has zillions of definitions, depending on the mental, emotional, or spiritual state of the definer. I liked this one today in relation to the dimensions of space and time of this particular moment.

Yes, every event in one's life is a story. Each life is a novel with all the stories put together, isn't it?

Let's pen down my own story. It is a story of a girl from a small town, a very small town, in Uttaranchal, which was carved out from the map of Uttar Pradesh a few years ago. It is where I grew up watching the crimson rays of the sun peep through my window every morning. I can still feel the icy-cold water splashed over my face by my ten little fingers, enough to make all my sensory nerve endings senseless. With the rising sun, nature would start revealing its beauty like a bride lifting her veil slowly, very slowly. The mesmerizing beauty is still in front of my eyes—the green hills, the white temple on one of those hilltops, the shimmery blue river arising from there and slowly disappearing somewhere. Huts getting lost in the heaps of houses—a sign of modernization.

And there was my house—number 49. This 'four plus nine equals thirteen' has a big role in my life. It may be unlucky for many, causing triskaidekaphobia (fear of number 13), but who cares? It's damn lucky for me!

For me, life took its first breath on the thirteenth day of May at the thirteenth hour. A second girl child was born when everybody was eagerly waiting for the cry of a baby boy. Does a baby boy cry a different cry? Does he smile differently? Or does he love his parents more? I still don't know. These questions used to haunt me a lot in my younger-hood. However, I have accepted the fact now that an XY birth is more welcomed in our civilized, modernized Indian society rather than an XX. Reasons are not one but many. Some concerns are defined, some anxieties are understood, and some fears are exemplified. However, most remonstrations stand vague in the umbra of social norms, culture, and traditions.

God has bestowed every girl with the energy to revamp the background. As a girl grows up, a new world vegetates with her. When she smiles in the depth of her sleep and when her granny joyfully exclaims that the little princess is still in her fairyland, all discriminations get washed off. Her soft tiny fingers, delicate sneezes, giggles, and her first footsteps start making a unique place for her in the vastness of this world. Love, affection, care, passion, and warmth become her exotic possessions.

The girl is leisurely growing up into a teenager and an adult. Beautiful she is at five feet six inches, with a slim and curvy torso bedecked with shoulder-length chocolate-brown curls, a round face subsuming two light-brown eyes, shadowed with long curved charcoal lashes, a sharp nose,

xii

prominent cheekbones, and supple lips wearing a stunning smile.

This is Riya, a grown-up Riya learning something new from life every day.

PART I

PART 1

Chapter 1

A Perfect Flirt

A beep sharply went inside and touched my heart.
Eyelids opened widely, lips stretched a little. I am sure it would have been a lovely smile. When a thought brightens your heart, each and every tiny cell of your body starts celebrating. That was what happened to me.

After a hectic day at the lab, I remember I just lay down to think of some beautiful things which started happening to me in the last four days, and dreaming about those things, I did not even realize when I fell asleep.

It was midnight here, pitch-dark and dead silent. My laptop showed 4 a.m. It was the time in India at the moment. I had not changed it since I had come here exactly three weeks ago—*Holland, the land of tulips, windmills, clogs, cheese, and tourists!*

Yes, it was exactly three weeks ago, a chilly winter morning when I landed here. Everyone around was draped in various shades of black, grey, blue, brown, and white. The only bright colour I could see was the one painted on my toenails, vibrant red. Other than this, life was really dull and colourless. This was my first opinion about Europe.

Standing at the prodigious Schiphol Airport with two heavy bags, I didn't know where to go. I felt it best to follow the crowd—walking belt, escalator, walking belt, wines, chocolates, diamonds, bags, clothes in the duty-free shops. Wow!

And finally, with the crowd, I reached at the immigration counter. 'Oh, Doctor? For six months! How come in Amsterdam?' a hefty white man asked.

'For research in cancer,' I replied.

'That's very nice. Good luck!'

A sensation of warmth gushed inside me in such a cold, colourless land.

I took my bulky bags from the conveyor belt number 11, put all things together in a trolley, and started my way to the exit, where the baggage checking was taking place. A young man who must be in his twenties took both my bags inside. I opened the bags with the combination 013.

'Very nicely arranged and packed,' he exclaimed. Firstly, I knew I wasn't very good in packing my bags, and secondly, whatever little I had done got topsy-turvy in such a long journey. But I smiled at the compliment, as by now I had already tasted a bit of the warm Dutch manner that made people comfortable. Then the same handsome guy helped me to buy my ticket to Sloterdijk—three euros and thirty cents (222 Indian rupees). My god! For the first time in my life, I thought that Indian autorickshaws were much better.

With difficulty, I dragged my two big black bags. I then noticed something that looked like a payphone out there. My eyes felt moist. I missed them all—my hubby the most, I guess. I desperately wanted him to be with me, but I knew that life is a journey which has to be traversed alone at times.

My laptop beeped again. I got up. The room was still dark, with a pinch of light getting sprinkled from my Facebook page. Without switching on any lights, I just sat on a small teapoy in front of the low table with my MacBook.

Why I felt I could watch this face till eternity, I do not know. There was nothing special about it—a long silent face with narrow eyes, sharp nose, small lips, a tuft of curly hair on top, and a thin layer of sparse hair on the cheeks and chin. This was definitely not what embezzled my heart away.

It was his words, I guess, which he never said and I never heard. It was what he wrote fifty-two hours ago and which I read more than a hundred times and repeated probably a billion times inside me: 'I will love you the way no one has ever loved anybody. Give me a chance.'

'Have you gone nuts? I am married.'

'Let us just chat only for the time you are there, away from home.'

I knew it was pure flirtation, but whatever it was, I was enjoying it. We chatted on Facebook every night for hours and hours together. I used to wait for it to become 8 p.m. in India—every day, every night.

'Hi, is someone there?' A new message flashed in front of my eyes, and the never-ending stories from Mumbai and Holland started once again that night.

I knew Neel only for the last ten days through Facebook. But it felt as if I knew him for ages. He happened to be a software engineer from Mumbai, single, simple, and lonely. Exactly opposite to me, who was ambitious, happily married, and happy!

So every moment I chatted with him, I reminded myself, 'It's a flirtation, just a flirtation.' For him to remember, after every few messages, I spoke about my family, my husband, his growing, expanding business, my in-laws, our marriage, and all those weird things an insecure married Indian girl can talk about.

And it seemed as if he enjoyed all of these—the foolishness and the weirdness—without any sign of jealousy or annoyance.

It was going on perfect for me—a perfect flirt in a cold and colourless country.

Chapter 2

What Seemed Colourless Was Not That Colourless Indeed!

The doorbell rang.

'Hi, James!' The voice was followed by one, two, and three loud kisses. I was sitting in the backyard with a mug of black coffee in my hands. I wanted to peep inside but was too shy even to look up. That's why Raghav calls me Pseudo. After doing everything happily, we Indian girls feel shy to talk about it. And there is nothing new; it has been the same for ages. In *Ramayana*, all the three queens of Dasaratha became pregnant after eating the holy kheer; Kauravas and Pandavas were born as the magical blessings of various gods. I believe nobody ever had sex in India. Still, it is the second most populated country.

'Hi. How's your day?' James asked me.

I had to come back to Holland from the land of *Ramayana* and *Mahabharata*. 'Yes, it was good,' I replied.

James was Anna's boyfriend. And Anna was the owner of this house, where I had rented a room for six months during my stay in Amsterdam—Sloterdijk 13-1, 1094 AX, Amsterdam, the Netherlands.

7

I was not in the mood to tell him my silly stories that morning—how I lost the sense of direction and came back to Sloterdijk three times, changing metros again and again just to discover that I was still standing at the same place where I was half an hour ago. Thank God, in Amsterdam you can travel anywhere with a single strip card within sixty minutes. You have to take a strip card (*strippenkaart*), which can be short or long, depending upon how long you want to use it. A long card has forty-five numbers in it, and the cost is twenty-one euros and sixty cents. Amsterdam is divided into zones. You have to calculate how many zones you will be crossing to reach the destination of your interest, fold the card till that number, and put it inside the small yellow machine. It will get stamped there with the exact time on it, and with that, you can travel any number of times you want to travel in a metro or a bus or a tram within that many zones. Nobody is there to check it, but you will find everybody stripping the card in. If the same system would have been in some other parts of the world, I can bet you, if not nine, eight out of ten people would have liked to travel either without the card or at least without stripping it.

At that moment, the three of us—Anna, James, and I—were here to make plans for the weekend. Out of the many attractions in the city—Keukenhof tulip garden, canal cruise, Van Gogh Museum, and many more—they settled for the famous red-light district and the adjoining green district for this Saturday.

'Amsterdam is one of those few unique cities in the world where prostitution is legal. Here the red-light district has existed since the fourteenth century,' the tour guide told us. He continued, 'This is the largest and most famous red-light area in Amsterdam and is known as De Wallen. The name Wallen [walls] refers to the medieval era dam walls erected in "old centrum" of Amsterdam.'

The red-light district is a famous tourist attraction, I realized. The streets were full of people with all sorts of dresses and appearances. We noticed the network of alleys having a number of one-room cabins rented by prostitutes, who exhibit themselves from behind windows or glass doors, typically illuminated with red lights. As I tried to click pictures, he warned me. 'It is not allowed here. If they see you clicking photos or making videos, they will snatch your cam and throw it in the canal in front of you. Be careful.'

'Prostitution has been legal in the Netherlands since 2000,' the guide informed.

'Didn't it exist before 2000? I think it had. I had come here earlier in the late nineties,' one of the middle-aged men from the crowd interrupted him suspiciously.

'Before 2000, prostitution was technically illegal although it existed more or less in the same illustrious form. By legalizing it, the government sought to gain more control of the industry and thereby bring an end to a range of abuses that had been occurring behind the curtains, like exploitation of children and forced prostitution. As the statistics reveals, with around 16 clubs and private houses, 25 escort agencies, 409 window brothels, having 7,000 women (and men) working as prostitutes, now things are more streamlined and in order in Amsterdam,' the guide continued with facts and figures.

We walked to the other side and crossed the canal. Our guide requested us to come together and started narrating another story. 'The green district of Amsterdam, having "coffee shops", has been a part of the city since the 1970s. Marijuana is technically illegal in the Netherlands, but possession of small amounts is not prosecuted, and it is sold openly in the coffee shops.'

'Something is not legal, and still, action is not taken by the police or the government when it is sold openly. This sounds weird,' I murmured.

The tour guide smiled. 'These coffee shops have always existed in a legal grey zone, selling the so-called soft drugs. Amsterdam's city council has an agreement with the coffee shop union known as Bond van Cannabis Detaillisten or BCD. This agreement allows coffee shops to operate with a non-transferable licence, shown by the display of an official green-and-white sticker in the window.'

'Can we try some?' one girl with an orange scarf on her head and holding hands with probably her boyfriend shouted. 'Yes. Why not? There are around two hundred such coffee shops in Amsterdam, and they can be identified easily with the green-and-white stickers in their windows. Even if you don't know anything about all this stuff, no issues, just go inside, and you will be provided with a menu. Don't hesitate to ask if you are not sure. Otherwise, you are in for a spin.' The guide winked.

'A rule of thumb,' James shouted from behind with a crooked smile on his lips, 'the more expensive it is, the stronger the weed. Keep in mind, gorgeous lady!'

My feet had started hurting, not because of walking but more because of the heels of my boots, so we decided to go home and have dinner there.

⊰⊱

Anna got a bottle of chilled white wine with some olives and cheese. She offered, but it was nice of her that she didn't force me. I had told her about what happened to me a week ago in a party which was organized to celebrate the promotion of one of the senior professors of the department of molecular pathology (where I had joined for my project). My colleagues were surprised when I told them that I had never tasted alcohol.

Susan asked me, 'Then what do you drink in India during your dinner?'

'Water!'

She thought for a while and whispered to herself, as if analysing in her deep thoughts, 'Oh, because people are poor there!' She turned and went to fill her glass again. She seemed to be satisfied with her reasoning, not really interested in my no, yes, or any explanation for that matter.

The two beautiful wine glasses touched each other, and they said, 'À la vôtre,' meaning 'cheers' in French. James is a French man, forty-four years old, separated from his wife four years ago. He has a thirteen-year-old son, Tim, who comes to stay with him during the weekends. Anna loves him like her own child, she told me. She met James around two years ago when she had got attracted to his naivety. I am sleeping with a multimillionaire these days. If you want, give me a call. This is my number. I will dump him tonight.' Before I could ask anything, she told me how it all began with James.

'Then?' I was too inquisitive to know.

'Then what? I dumped the millionaire.' She was too cool to kill my curiosity in just one go.

That was the real Holland—full of romance and full of broken hearts, full of parties and clubs, and full of loneliness and depression. A mix of red and green. I was learning it slowly. This place was so different from my India.

Chapter 3

Bubbles, Butterflies, and the Real World

Half past five, the alarm rang. I was off the bed, bathroom, dressing table, two slices of bread with cheese in the bag and two in hands, and I was ready to go to work.

It was six thirty-five sharp. I pulled my jacket from the peg behind the door, locked the door, and ran towards the station Sloterdijk. The morning was chilly. I hated not the cold but the harsh wind, which made my hair dry and rough. The timing was perfect. It had actually become perfect with the same practice again and again, day after day, now for nearly more than a month—last bite of my cheese sandwich and first step inside the station. Perfect!

I stripped in my card and climbed towards the *metrolijn* 50 (the green line) for Amstelveenseweg. This route took hardly seven to eight minutes, after which I had to walk around five hundred metres to reach the front gate of CCA (Cancer Centre Amsterdam). The perspicuous blue-and-red blocked building of CCA, which is the heart of cancer research in VU Medical Centre, is certainly difficult to be missed by anyone. Inside those blue-and-red blocks, around five hundred researchers are striving hard every day to find out solutions to prevent, diagnose, treat, and cure human cancers.

I preferred the backdoor, which required an identity chip card for the entry. It opened directly to the third floor, where the cervical cancer group was located. The backdoor entry took five minutes lesser to take me inside my lab, and I loved this, as much as I loved my work. Most of the days, I used to be the first one to enter and the last one to leave the lab. My passion drove me to come here even on Saturdays and Sundays.

To work in the area of cancer was my eternal desideratum. De facto the first moment I became aware that we all have to have an ambition to become something in life, I wished to become a doctor, so as to be able to lend a hand to cure, to mellow out someone's suffering, to eliminate an ailment. However, there is a hidden secret that I have never shared with anybody till this moment. Even before the wish to become a doctor mushroomed inside, I had a secret dream in life. I wanted to become a bride, a beautiful one, even without knowing what it actually meant. Although my mind started evolving, moods started changing, thoughts started maturing, and I started dreaming of bigger things in life something as great as eliminating all the sufferings of humankind, still the dream of becoming a bride of a charming prince never could fade away. I remember when I was ten, my mind calculated that exactly eight years later I would be celebrating the long-awaited moment of my life. I had come across an advertisement sponsored by the government of India on television promoting the age of marriage in India for girls as eighteen. My tiny neurons took it quite seriously, imagining that according to the rule, all girls in India should get married on their eighteenth birthday.

As time passed by, in my mind, some pictures became bigger and brighter at the expense of other dreams and memories, which kept on shrinking. In the bargain of accommodating new dreams, my eighteenth, nineteenth, twentieth birthday passed on. In the fight of small and big dreams, dreams started getting compromised to conveniences. I settled for biotechnology studies when I couldn't get a medical seat. Synchronically, I forgot about my Prince Charming riding his white horse. Having finished my graduate and post-graduate studies in biotechnology a month after my twenty-fourth birthday, I got enrolled for PhD. All credits to my dynamic guide, Professor Shivshankar Thakur, I completed my PhD in four years and ten months. Under his guidance, I worked in the field of cell regeneration and cell line production. We generated sixteen animal cell lines, which could be utilized for research to mimic damage and repair system in human tissues. In June 2008, I was awarded PhD for the same work.

Soon after, it was like a dream come true when I received the Marie Curie International Fellowship in Holland. I had got the opportunity to work in the area of cervical oncogenes and oncogenesis in a centre which was famous for its breakthrough research by Professor Walboomer and his group. They were the first to demonstrate that 99.7 per cent (that is almost all) of cervical cancer cases are caused by a virus known as HPV (human papillomavirus). Their results wobbled up the medical as well as the research fraternity across the globe. Discovering the presence of HPV in virtually all cervical cancer cases implied that we now knew the highest attributable fraction for a specific cause of any major human cancer so far reported. This report changed the so-far-hypothesized natural history of cervical cancer, where the blame was on multiple vague factors like early menarche, early marriage, early childbirth, late menopause, poor hygiene, and likewise. Now cervical cancer meant having HPV as the root cause.

For obvious reasons, a lot of HPV-related research was ongoing in this department of CCA, now headed by Professor Herrington. This included HPV in cervical carcinogenesis, HPV with or without genetic epigenetic markers, HPV in chromosomal chaos, HPV in many other permutations and combinations.

I was fortunate to get one of the best group leaders anyone can ever experience or even imagine, Debora A. M. Snijders, a five-foot-three-inch-tall lady in her forties, with blonde pixie-cut hair, grey eyes, and pronounced grace. She was the right hand of Professor Herrington. For me, Debora was more like a friend or sister rather than a boss. She not only helped me a lot to get adjusted to this new working environment, but she also was a perpetual guide for dos and don'ts at every possible front since the day I decided to come here. I was allotted Group C2, where my specific project included identification of methylation markers in cervical cancer, pre-cancerous as well as normal tissues which were infected with HPV.

Today I was supposed to process thirty-six new samples collected last month as a part of routine screening. I applaud and I salute to such nationwide, well-organized system of cervical cancer screening in Holland, which is totally free of cost. Debora explained, 'Each year, about eight hundred thousand women receive invitation for a Pap smear. As soon as a woman in Holland celebrates her thirtieth birthday, she receives this invitation, which means that she has to meet a GP now and take an appointment for her test. In this way, every woman between thirty and sixty years who can have this test.'

'And what if the lady is not able to come because of any reason? May it be health, distance, social and family related responsibilities, as happens most of the time in India. Will they miss the chance to get screened?' I asked.

'Maybe not, because there is a provision of getting a self-sampling kit also. If you are not able to visit a doctor for any reason, you will be sent a kit by post. As per the instructions, the sample has to be collected and posted back to the lab.'

She continued, 'CCA is currently striving hard to optimize this screening programme with addition of high-risk HPV testing to the Pap test with the same sample. This is known as co-testing and theoretically supposed to improve the efficacy of Pap test. Group A1 presently is working for the same hypothesis. With their preliminary results, it looks like soon this concept will replace the present screening programme, at least in the Netherlands.'

In this country, even after having such screening programmes, 200–250 women die of cervical cancer every year, I had read somewhere. I can't figure out what was happening back home, with such a population, poverty, and unawareness, amalgamated with the frigid attitude of Indian government in this issue.

Curiosity dragged me to look up the figures, and it was tragic to explore that in my country, 70,000 women die every year because of cervical cancer. Every seven minutes, this cruel disease kills one woman in India. If you see, this is much higher than the more commonly spoken and politically used/misused topics in my motherland. The statistics narrates one dowry death in India every ninety-three minutes and one maternal death every ten minutes. There are hundreds of rules, regulations, legislations, and facilities to reduce such mishaps. But what is our government doing to reduce the incidence of dying women due to a cancer, which is totally preventable? Having known this, all my feelings suddenly swapped from the ecstasy I felt to learn about the Hollandian way of screening to the distressing facts and figures of cervical cancer statistics in my own country. I am agonized. I am oppressed.

Oh, it was already nine twenty. I was sitting and wondering in front of the computer. I realized when Debora came and asked me, 'Where are your samples?'

'Give me ten minutes, please.' I took my empty sample box and ran down the stairs to reach the basement behind the parking lot, where very methodically, in around eight huge freezers, samples from patients were stored at minus twenty degrees Celsius. I opened the fourth freezer from the left, which was labelled CxCy02-08 in the 4F tray and took out those thirty-six samples which I was supposed to analyse today. I read the identification numbers on my list and took out the sample from the tray. The samples were so systematically organized that it took me hardly fifteen minutes to collect them and get back to the lab.

I placed the samples outside in a stand and, meanwhile, kept all the things required for the DNA extraction ready with Reni's (the lab assistant) help. She was waiting for me with around fifty other samples from some other groups to be processed with my samples. The first time I saw the robot extracting DNA here, I was thrilled. Robotic DNA extraction not only reduces the hands-on time but also the probability of manual errors. Robotic revolution has begun from cleaning your room to serving you food and from handling DNA to performing surgeries. Robots are ready to handle anything and everything now.

While I finished yesterday's pending documentation, planned for next day's work, had a cup of coffee with friends, and ate a delicious marble cake brought by Debora, the robot darling had extracted all the DNA perfectly. I took out my thirty-six samples, labelled the tubes, placed it in a new tray, and kept it in the first fridge at four degrees Celsius in the lab. It was now ready to be analysed tomorrow for HPV. It was already twenty minutes past three in the afternoon, and we had a group meeting at half past three.

Quickly I went to the canteen, grabbed some salad, and ran towards the meeting room. Every Thursday, all of us sat together here to discuss work done this week and to plan the next week. It was planned in the meeting that next week I should also go to the histopathology section to slice the tissue paraffin blocks, make fresh slides, stain those, and keep them ready for DNA extraction from disease-specific areas. After the meeting was over, I made a telephonic appointment with histology section chief, Dr Bart, for Monday morning.

My day was done at work. The wall clock announced five. I was hungry, and I was tired.

I took off my lab coat, wore my jacket, wrapped on the muffler, and ran towards the metro station. At exactly five forty, I was home. I switched on the heating system, made some India masala Maggi, and ate it alone . . . all alone . . . with some Dutch reality show on television, without a meaning to me.

The reason for working late and on weekends might be other than the passion too. With my family being in India and not having many friends here, I had enough and more time for work. In India, for most of the working places, Saturday is also a working day, so indirectly, this so-called overenthusiastic extra work was indeed filling the emptiness of this time lag for me.

And yes, Neel was also a busy software professional working for Oracle, which he had joined recently under a draconian boss, but still, he could manage to spare hours together with me. I appreciate it.

It took me two minutes to prepare my Maggi and one minute to finish it. I washed my bowl and fork and sneaked inside the cosy quilt. In less than a few seconds, I was out, I guess. At 8 p.m., like every day, I was alerted by my iPhone alarm, which, unlike mornings, I never used to snooze.

I was fresh. Quickly I switched on the laptop and read this: 'Sorry, won't be able to talk to you tonight. Have to go for a friend's birthday party. Tried to make hundreds of excuses, but they are not ready to listen to anything. I am really sorry. Please understand.'

My face fell, and with a gloomy hand, I scrolled down.

But maybe I can use this opportunity to tell you something which I will never be able to tell you face to face (I mean Facebook to Facebook) when we are *sitting together*, deceiving the dimensions of time and space on either side of Facebook.

I won't be able to tell you that . . .

The curve of your cheeks,
The shine of the brown of your eyes,
The curls of your hair,
The smile on your lips,
Is enough to make me crazy!

The bambino in your thoughts,
The chuckle in your words,
The passion in your dreams,
The ecstasy in your flirt too . . .
Trust me . . . Is making me go crazy.

I felt like crying, crying aloud. Where were you five years ago? I missed him like I have never missed anybody ever.

Chapter 4

Celebration of Life

D o you know that 'love' is one among the most-searched words in Google? To my surprise, it was searched 20,634 times last year, yet it remains enigmatic, inscrutable.

Unlike the childhood aspirations, when I reached the eighteenth year of my life, I was busy sorting out my career plan and had possibly forgotten about my presumptions about the age of marriage in India. Life was going on hectic; when I couldn't clear medical entrance in first attempt, there was a lot of pressure from Dad not to waste time further. As a result, I joined BSc in biotechnology, which was followed by MSc and PhD. There was nothing much to think about other than work, study, presentations, and deadlines.

Just a month had passed since I got enrolled for my PhD, Dipa Mausi (Mom's younger sister) came with what Mom says 'the best marriage proposal' for me. Dad wanted his daughter to take the final decision, so I planned to meet him.

I wore a pink full-sleeved *chikankari kurti* elegantly hugging my curves with black leggings and black chunni. I added pearl and silver danglers to my ears, outlined my eyes with kohl, and carefully glued a small black *bindi* exactly in the middle of my eyebrows. I decided to keep my shoulder-length curls to remain open for the special evening. With a light spray of my favourite Eternity Moments by Calvin Klein, I was ready.

Smiti, my childhood friend, was waiting outside for me in her car. We drove towards the CCD, where we had decided to meet Raghav. We both recognized him as we had seen his pics many, many times before. Around six feet two inches tall, Raghav was sitting on a red couch in his white T-shirt and blue denim.

'He looks even more handsome in person than his snapshots, isn't he?' Smiti whispered.

On seeing us, he got up, welcomed us with a warm smile, and handed over a pack of chocolates to Smiti before giving me a lovely bunch of white lilies. I was impressed, and so was she, I guess.

He ordered a lemonade and corn–spinach sandwich. Smiti ordered strawberry slush and a brownie, while I was too nervous to order anything other than a cup of hot coffee.

He spoke less and analysed more. Smiti was the chatterbox. I think I stood somewhere in between these two extremes. Raghav told us about his business and his small company, his showrooms, his busy schedule, his parents, who lived in Kanpur, and his younger sister Vartika, who was studying in the DU (Delhi University).

Smiti divulged stories of our childhood friendship and her insecurities about someone new intruding into that space, then about her medical-school life, her ambition to become a cosmetologist and earn a lot of money, and blah-blah.

As my PhD was ongoing, I could think only of that. Whether it was my dedication or nervousness of the moment, God only knows!

But one thing I realized in these one and a half hours was that Raghav was a living example of a descent and well-mannered boy. Mom and Mausi were right. It was a good option to consider him.

It was time to bid bye for today. Raghav hugged Smiti gently but affectionately. Then he stretched his hand towards me and said, 'You take your time to decide. It's yes from my side!'

He escorted us to the area in the parking lot where Smiti had parked her car. He opened the door for me and waited there till we drove away.

'I am not taking you home. I want parrrttty!' Smiti almost shouted as soon as he was out of our sight.

I blushed but said, 'I have not yet decided, darling.'

Smiti burst into laughter. 'Shut up, okay! I know you more than you know yourself.'

'Okay, I promise you, we will go for a grand party. But please take me home now. I want to share everything with Mom. I am sure Dad will be very happy.' I felt a weird kind of amusement inside.

This day onwards, as if time seemed to grow wings, I did more dreaming and shopping than chatting and meeting Raghav. Most of the time, either he was too busy or too tired. But in only a few days, life was about to change. All the dreams were waiting to come true. It was a matter of only few months now.

After five days of elaborate celebrations of a grand Indian wedding, on 13 December we two individuals were a couple.

With four months of planning and preparations, it all started on the 9th, with the ring ceremony, mehndi, sangeet, and tilak, one after the other. It was a complete festivity with music, dance, jokes, lights, camera, sweets, flowers, and a lot more actions. My whole family from my mom's side and dad's side had come as I was the youngest among all the cousins. All of them (total of twelve) were married and had one or two numero unos each. Neeraj *bhaiya*, my *tauji*'s son, was an exception. He lived in Phoenix, Arizona, USA, and decided not to marry. The reason was not known to anyone, and none of us dared to ask it ever, as he was the eldest and eremitic.

I would say that 13 December was a day of an emotional admixture and conflict. I felt euphoric, nostalgic, happy, blessed, melancholic, anxious, embarrassed, and spiritual all at a same time.

The pandit jee said something first in Sanskrit and translated it on behalf of Raghav, I guess, while the two of us circled the Agni (holy fire).

> I am the sky, you are the earth. I am the thought,
> > you are the speech.
> I am the fire and you are the fuel. I am the song,
> > you are the verse.
> I am the ocean, you are the shore. I am the strength
> > but you are the beauty.

The other pandit jee made us repeat after him the seven marriage vows with seven steps.

With the first step, we will provide for and support each other.

With the second step, we will develop mental, physical, and spiritual strength.

With the third step, we will share the worldly possessions.

With the fourth step, we will acquire knowledge, happiness, and peace.

With the fifth step, we will raise strong and virtuous children.

With the sixth step, we will enjoy the fruits of all seasons.

With the seventh step, we will always remain friends and cherish each other.

I entered the beautifully decorated room on the second floor with Vartika, my official sister-in-law now. Having oriented me to the geography of the room, she smiled and left.

I took off my glamorous jewellery, changed my dress, had a relaxing bubble bath, and wore the beautiful lilac gown which I had chosen after rejecting almost a hundred night gowns. I had no make-up and no jewellery this time. I had enough of it in the last five days. I pulled back all my hair together to bring it to the right side of my neck. It still smelt pretty. Mirror whispered, 'You look perfect, perfect for this night!'

He knocked on the door and came inside in white kurta pyjamas with a bottle of Coke in his left hand and a box of chocolates in the right one. He kept both inside the small fridge, which was placed in a shelf on the far left corner of the room. He placed his Samsung Galaxy Grand on the side table for charging, then held my hand and brought me to the bed. 'Are you tired?'

Though I was from head to toe, I shook my head from side to side, meaning 'no'.

And it followed—love and love and love . . .

Having had two beautiful honey-kissed rounds of lovemaking, I was lying so close to him that I could not only count but even follow the rhythm of his *lub-dub*. His fingers were gently caressing my bare back. Both of us were sleepy but not yet sleeping.

His Galaxy Grand vibrated, once, twice, and thrice.

He got up and stretched his hand to pick the phone. I too got up, thinking, *It must be an emergency. So late in the night, that too today!* I switched on the table lamp.

He just held the phone in his hands and did not receive the call. It was still vibrating. It looked as if it was a call from an unknown number, and Raghav was trying to remember who it could be.

But no, the screen had a name. It read 'Sara calling'. He cut the call. Put it back to charge. Turned his back towards me and slept off.

I followed the same.

Chapter 5

Life Is in Turmoil

Life was going on good—parties with family and friend, gifts, and blessings. As the days kept on moving forward, the guest crowd at home started thinning and diluting.

Two weeks were over so fast. We had to leave for Mumbai two days later, where I would be continuing my PhD. My darling hubby had decided to continue his business from his Mumbai office till my PhD was finished, and for which, there were still at least four years. Plan after that was not yet decided.

Raghav had already arranged an apartment there which was close to my institution. After around a month, in the first week of January, I decided to go back to work. So did he.

Life became more or less the same routine—getting up, getting ready, breakfast in a hurry. Day was full of work and work. Both of us used to get late for coming back. Reasons were many for me—ongoing experiments, meetings, preparations for presentations. For him, it was only one—Mumbai traffic. However, Raghav was not in Mumbai most of the time because of his business deals.

I wanted to spend more and more time with him and enjoy my life, but it was not happening the way I had dreamt it. Both of us most of the days were worked up with our own things, so trivial fights were common—like what usually happens in any married life, I agree and understand!

But my problem was something else. If we had some conflict, I wanted him to fight with me and sort it out. Instead, he would take his keys and leave the house, leaving me frustrated, irritated, agitated, and maybe depressed.

Days turned into nights; weeks melted into months and years. I got adjusted to life, and life got adjusted to me.

In the fall of 2008, I submitted my thesis-writing. A few days later, Professor Thakur called me and said, 'Now you have, say, some three-odd months till your thesis defence. I give you two options. Whichever you want to choose, it is entirely up to you.'

It was unexpected of him to give options. I had worked under him for more than four years. I knew there was only one way to accomplish things, and that was *his* way. I thought they say in science, 'Nothing is yes, and nothing is no.' Today's yes might be tomorrow's no or vice versa. A scientist has to be very open-minded and an out-of-the-box thinker. However, none of these rules applied to Prof. Shivshankar Thakur.

He continued, 'Option one: You have worked hard all these years. Take your leave and go to your parents, or go for an outing with your husband and enjoy life. And option two: Apply for this.' He gave me a cover torn off from one side with around four printed A4 papers inside.

I tried to pull out the papers from the cover to see what it was. He interrupted, 'Not now. Go home, relax, discuss it with your family, and let me know. Anyways, even if your answer is no, these papers are waste for me, as I don't think other than you in my department anyone else is worthy of having this.'

A million choco balls started bursting and melting inside my heart. *This man, whose inspirations are tongue-lashings, whose agitation is tearing off papers, whose appreciation is more work for next week, had said this to me today? He feels I am a deserving candidate and I am the only one who deserves something which is inside the envelope.* I got goosebumps all over my body. Still, I didn't know what was inside it.

I went straight to my cubicle, and there was the form for the very, very prestigious Marie Curie International (postdoctoral) Fellowship. Not applying for this was not an option. I was happy—the happiest soul in this world.

The next moment, I thought of Raghav. He would definitely say no. Definitely. He would have made plans once I finished my PhD. After marriage till date, my life had not been milk and honey as I had dreamt it. Maybe I was not able to give him enough time. I blamed myself.

Then suddenly my thought wave drifted to these four years, which flew away with a supersonic rustle. *Raghav has been so tolerant, so tolerant despite of my mood swings now and then. He has been very supportive. I am fortunate to have him,* I thought. *Now, it's my turn to prove myself.* At this point in time, diving deep in the ocean of heartfelt emotions, I wanted to be a good wife and nothing else. My love-dipped heart echoed inside, *Forget all the reasons why it won't work and believe the one reason why it will.*

I left the papers on my table and walked towards home. While on the way, I planned a perfect evening, with life's best dinner and everything best following that.

———◆———

It was 7 p.m., and I was ready!

Today, dinner had sago cutlets as starters, with mint chatni, *masala paneer*, *bhindi*, *chapatti*, and *jeera rice*, followed by *gulab jamuns* as dessert.

Each and every item in the menu was Raghav's favourite. It took me more than five hours to prepare them all with the help of Dipika Nehlani's cookbook and Google.

Being the youngest in the entire family, I was the pampered and the spoiled one. I never learnt cooking from Mom. Whenever Dipa Mausi commented, 'Riya, learn something. How will you cook for your husband after you marriage?' I sternly and confidently replied, 'Mausi, don't you know that I will marry a multimillionaire prince? There will be chefs to cook, and yes, I will feed my prince with my lovely delicate hands.' Mausi and Mom used to get irritated, though my dad always laughed at this and seemed proud of me.

Anyways, those were childhood tales. Today the day had come for me to cook lovely dinner for my Prince Charming with my own lovely hands. But yes, like the food, I should also look attractive. I wrapped shimmer of my aquamarine sari around me which was Raghav's wedding anniversary gift this year, added a bindi on my forehead, did a bit of eyes, and wore my fragrance.

Just then, the bell rang, and I could read the surprise on Raghav's face. Whether it was more in his eyes, which was looking at me, or his nose, which was trying to smell something, I couldn't tell indubitably.

After he changed, I served him food. He took the first bite of sago cutlet and gave a look full of umbrage. I was surprised.

'What's this, Riya? It's so damn salty. Why do you have to experiment with me? That too at dinner time.'

I looked down towards my plate so that he didn't see my wet eyes. The drops were ready to fall down any moment.

He ate some chapattis and rice, all in silence. Thinking that his mood had become better now, I passed him the bowl of gulab jamuns.

He cut a piece out of one of the jamuns with difficulty and then left it with fork still in its heart. He stood and went straight towards the bedroom.

I went inside the bathroom, cried, sobbed, came out, and entered the bedroom. It seemed Raghav was already asleep, or at least he was pretending so.

I also changed and slipped inside the quilt.

Not all scars are seen
Not all wounds will heal
How to show you the loneliness
Which deep inside my heart I feel!

Morning at the breakfast, I told him that Professor Thakur called me for the fellowship but that I had decided not to go and had planned to inform the professor today of my decision.

To my surprise, Raghav held my hand, smiled, and said, 'I think you must not miss this opportunity.' He paused and kissed my hand. 'I am sorry for last night, Riya. I was tired.'

———— ❖ ————

I was happy, but I was puzzled.

I decided to talk to my mom as usual in the moments of crises and confusion.

'Riya, you must go, I feel,' she said after listening to my whole story patiently.

'Are you sure, Maa?' At least I was not sure.

She tried to explain her rationale. 'Look, Riya, Raghav is doing very good in his career. He has taken his small family business to admirable international heights.'

'Hmm.' I knew this well. No doubts in that.

'Ours is a middle-class family, Riya. Your education and your career are your only strength. If you do not progress ten year down the line, he will blame you that he always encouraged you but you were lazy to progress in life. I feel you should at least try.'

I understood. 'You are right, Mama. I will surely try. Try with my whole heart and soul. I have let go of many things, many dreams in life. Not this one!'

I put the phone down and told myself, 'Riya Goyal, you have to prove yourself. You might be a horrible cook, but you can definitely do better things in life!'

Chapter 6

The Virtual Parties

I was one among the fortunate ones to receive the fellowship.

I reached Amsterdam on 10 January. Full of enthusiasm, I went to CCA the very day. Life was so different here for me—lots of work, new friends, new culture, and loneliness.

On 5 February, when I was just rewinding my life story in my own flashback, sipping a cup of black coffee, I saw a friend request from India. I was missing India so badly at that moment that without seeing the other details, I clicked Accept.

Ten minutes later, a message flashed on my Facebook screen.

'Hi, Riya! I can see your institute from my office window.'

It was stupid. I didn't bother to answer.

'I think I can see you. Are you the one in blue top? I am still at work, doing some stupid job for a US project. Getting bored.'

I was about to shut down my computer.

'I am sorry if you didn't like the joke. By the way, I am Neel, a software engineer working for Oracle Mumbai, very close to your JLN Institute of Life Sciences.'

Just to stop him, I typed, 'Sorry, but I don't live in Mumbai now. I am in Amsterdam.'

'Wow. That's amazing. Can we chat for a while? If it's okay with you.'

'Actually I was searching for an old childhood friend, Riya Goyal, and came across your profile. The bird in the display picture is so attractive. I was wondering if birds can also make profiles in FB. Just to confirm, I sent you a request.'

'Bad joke . . .' I replied with a smiley.

'I know it's a PJ, but see, at least it made you smile.'

'By the way, I would like to tell you that I am married,' rudely I wrote.

'Ha ha ha, thanks for the kind information.'

'Anyways, it's my sleeping time. Goodnight.' I logged off without bothering to see the reply.

Next morning, as soon as I got up, I opened the laptop to see if Raghav had left a message for me. But what I got was this:

Riya, I don't know why I messaged you, but when I did, I didn't expect a reply. But you replied. Whatever small chat we had, I enjoyed the feeling. Today, I don't know why all this happened, but I am a strong believer in coincidence and destiny.

Eventually, all pieces fall into place.
Until then . . .
Laugh at the confusion, live for the moment.
And know that everything happens for a reason.

And like this, it all started. Every night we chatted—me and Neel (the guy I had never met in real).

Raghav's mails and messages were reducing from twice a day to once a day, to twice a week, and now to once a week.

Actually, now even I didn't care. I had a company, in a virtual world though, with whom I could share, I could laugh, and I could cry without having the fear of being judged.

'What's for dinner tonight, madam?' he asked.

'Today? Only yogurt.'

'I feel like having a pizza, but I need your company.'

'Okay, I am ready, but how?'

He laughed. 'By chance, a delivery boy of Pizza Hut happens to be a good friend. If you can give your address, I will request him to deliver it to you. Simple, but I will need your address, madam!' It was a game.

I was in a good mood. I said, 'Sure. You may please note it down. It's Sloterdijk 13-1, 1094 AX, Amsterdam.'

We kept on laughing. We kept on chatting.

My doorbell rang. 'It must be Anna. I need to go.'

'Okey-dokey. I will wait.' I read this and left the room, as the bell rang once, twice, and thrice.

To my surprise, it was not Anna but a boy with a red cap on his head and a blue-and-white box in his hands. 'Your order, ma'am.'

It took me a second to realize what had happened. I took the box and ran towards my room.

I read, 'My pizza has also come now. We can eat together. With your kind permission, madam.'

My eyes became wet, but my lips smiled. Nobody had cared for me so much even in the same house. Whether I ate my dinner or not, no one was bothered. And here was someone who cared so much for me, sitting thousands of miles away. Was it a dream? No, it couldn't be, because this was something which I couldn't have imagined even in my dreams. And this was the tastiest pizza I ever had in my life.

There were surprises . . . every day.

We went in an imaginary road trip to Goa. We shared music. We shared pictures. We even had my birthday bash. We cut the fake cake. He sang 'Happy Birthday to You' and smeared the cream on my face. We had a candle-lit dinner. When I asked for my birthday present, he asked me to close my eyes, and when I was instructed to open them, I got this.

Happy birthday to a lovely friend.
Let our friendship always ascend.
On me, you may always depend.
I want you to feel proud at the end.

What we share is such a weird trend.
In front of you, I never pretend.
More time now if I don't spend,
Six month later, I am going to repent.

On the next day, I told him, 'Neel, I feel we should stop this now. Sometimes I feel I am cheating on my husband!'

'Listen to me, Riya! Do you trust me? I promise you, once you are back in India, I will never talk to you. Only for six months, till you are here. We are not doing anything wrong.'

'Are you sure?'

'Yes, I am, and trust me, I will never let you fall. I respect your emotions. I respect your feeling. I respect you the way you are.'

'Thank you.'

'If you feel it's okay, I want to see you once in person—only once, I promise. If you don't want to meet me, even if it is to see you from far away somewhere, I am fine with that too.'

Without expectations, without judgements, life was *fun*!

This virtual world was better than the real one.

Chapter 7

A Queen Is a Queen

Even the real world had offbeat wonders and thrills for me in Holland. Today I was trying to search for an orange dress, but except of this dress with a few tiny orange patches, I couldn't figure out anything else to wear.

The whole nation was supposed to be painted in orange today. Exciting! It was 30 April and a national holiday in the Netherlands.

Debora, Anna, James, and almost everybody had apprized me that it was something which should not be missed. Anna and James wanted me to accompany them, but their plans were huge—partying late night and staying at some friend's farmhouse afterwards. As for me, some fixed hours in the evening had become so crucial that whatever happened, I wanted to be home from 6 to 10 p.m. without any excuse.

I asked Anna, 'What's so great about your Queen's Day? Do you still have a real queen?'

She smiled and gave me a booklet from her shelf. 'You can read everything here. James and Tim are waiting for me. I will have to leave now, darling.'

I shut the door behind her and went to my room. It didn't take me more than ten minutes to go through the pages of that information booklet.

In short and simple, the story goes like this: The Queen's Day is celebrated in the whole Netherlands since more than a hundred years. During the 1880s, the Liberal Union of Holland, which was part of the government, made a plan to promote national unity. As their King William III was not liked by many, they planned to launch Princess Wilhelmina, who was just four years that time, for the same. It was proposed that the princess's birthday be celebrated as an opportunity for patriotic celebration and national reconciliation.

Princess's Day was first celebrated in the Netherlands on 31 August 1885, on Wilhelmina's fifth birthday. The young princess was paraded through the streets, waving to the crowds. The celebration became popular and continued every year. The trend was followed. As the young princess grew up, it was renamed as the famous Queen's Day.

The trend has been going on like this. In the modern days, Koninginnedag celebration here has become the world-famous orange craze. The colour orange is a ubiquitous sight: orange banners, orange food, orange drinks, orange hats, and orange clothes. It's a day of festivity, magnanimous parties, loud music, and not to be forgotten, free markets (*vrijmarkt*), which are spread in almost all the streets.

And here I was the next morning, ready to join the orange craze in my multicoloured midi with a few orange patches and black knee-length boots. Though the air felt warm today, I sensed it was wise to keep my coat with me, having had a few bad experiences with weather prediction in the past.

When I had come here, I felt it funny that everyone talks about the weather. One of the most important topics of discussion, I realized, in Europe was 'weather'. In India, the weather usually is so predictable that people don't bother even to talk about it. We know our seasons, and we know the weather.

I took the metro green line (number 50) to Zuid, changed to orange line (number 81) to enter the Orange World in the Centrum (most happening area of Amsterdam). It looked like it had rained orange here. Everything was drenched in orange—orange hair, orange caps, orange faces, orange masks, orange T-shirts. Few of the people had even orange pants and orange shoes. I saw two huge German shepherds wrapped in orange frills. There were orange banners, orange balloons, orange flags, and orange boat with orange people on the canal. Believe it or not, it was *oranjegekte* (orange craze) indeed.

It was more orange what I have seen in toto till today in my entire lifetime!

I entered the crowd and got lost in the magic of celebration.

Suddenly there was a hustle, a palpable discomfort or anxiety in the crowd. People left the crowd, stood on the sides in groups, and started discussing some serious matter.

I was puzzled. Whom to ask? What to ask?

I also left the crowd, intuiting that something had seriously gone wrong. I stopped at a Dutch *pannenkoeken* (pancake) stall and asked a waiter there. He replied, 'News is that there was a terror attack on the queen today. So mostly all the celebrations and parties are being cancelled.'

'Oh, hope the queen is safe!' instantly it came out of my mouth.

He smiled an inch and said, 'By God's grace, yes, she is! However some other people are seriously injured.' Then he left, keeping my pancakes elegantly on my table with a small jar of honey.

I roamed around, on the bridges, around the city, near the canals, but the feeling had become gloomy, and I planned to leave.

———◈———

Anna opened the door and nearly screamed at me, 'Listen to me, Riya. Tomorrow after work, you are coming with me to buy a phone and a SIM card. Do you understand?'

'Why, what happened?' I exclaimed.

'You know your people are so worried about you, and there was no way to contact you.'

'Why? What happened? Can I come inside?'

Still standing on the door, she gave me some place to slide in.

As the parties were cancelled and the atmosphere has become hostile, James and Anna also had returned.

I took a seat on the dining table next to James. Anna poured me coffee. 'You know your husband is so worried. He came to know about the attack, and he had called me ten times since then.'

'Who, Raghav?'

'No, his friend, I guess, Neel. That's what he said, I guess.'

'Oh, is it? They must be worried. I will first send a message and then join you in five minutes.' I rushed towards my room.

I opened Internet, and there were I don't know how many messages from Neel and only Neel. I didn't read it but just replied, 'I am perfectly fine. Will chat with you in half an hour.'

I climbed down to join James and Anna. We had coffee and some chit-chat, but my heart was in India—whether with Raghav, to find out if he knew about the news, or with Neel, thinking about how much he cares, I don't know. It was difficult to answer.

In twenty to twenty-five minutes (definitely less than thirty) as I went back to my laptop, Neel was already online.

'Hey, where were you? I was so worried about you.'

'Why? I am not the Queen of Holland!'

'For me, you are not less than that.'

Before I could react, he wrote, 'Just kidding.'

'I saw the clip in the news,' he said. 'Who was that mad guy?'

'I don't know. But people are saying he can't be a terrorist. He was all alone, and he was seriously injured. He has been taken to the hospital.'

'Six or seven other people also got seriously injured. One lady succumbed on the spot. They showed it in BBC and all the other channels too. I got really worried about you.'

'I am in Amsterdam. The accident happened in Apeldoorn, a different town.'

'You are a crazy girl. Who knows, you could have reached there too to see the queen.' It sounded like a cute sarcasm.

'Luckily, nothing happened to the queen and her family, but all parties have been cancelled here.'

'That's obvious.'

'Hey, they are showing the queen on TV.'

I increased the volume and indulged in the queen and her statement. I forgot that I was in a chat.

'Hey, that queen is safe. You come here. I am missing my queen so badly.'

I smiled and didn't say anything to him on this. I just changed the topic and stared conversing as I didn't read it.

Chapter 8

Inquisitiveness

'Will it be painful? Is there a chance that I start bleeding?'

I came with my coffee mug to join them during the morning break.

Oho, so gossip about the first night is going on. Interesting! my Indian mind thought.

But by the time I settled myself next to Rene, having pulled a chair from the other table, I realized that it was not about what I was thinking. Elsa Steenbergen had received an invite to attend the cervical cancer screening programme, and the appointment was in the afternoon today after one month of her thirtieth birthday.

Everyone around there was sharing their opinions and experiences about the Pap test. Debora said, 'When I had the test for the first time, the gynaecologist, her gloved hand, and her metallic instruments appeared so scary that I started counting all my boyfriends till then and started cursing them one by one.'

Rene started laughing hysterically. 'Debora, at least you could remember all of them. I don't even remember how many!'

'My gynaecologist is the best. He is so gentle. He is so handsome. If he is made in charge to take Pap smear for everybody, I am sure our screening programmes will become 100 per cent successful, and nobody will ever die of cervical cancer in Holland,' Isabella confessed.

I had no story to share. I had never discussed any such thing with anybody except once with Smiti. Smiti was in her final year of medical school that time and was posted in the department of gynaecology (OBG) those days.

She told me how a gynaecologist does pelvic examination. 'Looking at the perineum of women all the time. Yuck! A gynaecologist's job is so dirty.'

I always had great respect for doctors. I was surprised. 'Don't talk like this, Smiti.'

'I am not joking, Riya,' Smiti tried to explain. 'They live a shitty life, these gynaecologists and obstetricians. Their life is soaked in blood, urine, meconium, and what not. It is limited to a two centimetre opening at the bottom.' She laughed loudly. 'I will never take gynaecology.' She grimaced.

'Do you know what Sameer Chaddha that Delhi boy was saying today? These gynaec mams might not remember the names and faces of their patients, but once they peep in their bottoms, they will be able to say, "Oh, you are Seeta, and you are Geeta!"'

'Really!' I exclaimed. 'You talk like this about your teachers?'

'Whatever, Riya, I want to swear in front of you today. I can take any branch but not gynaecology.'

'Yeah, I know, my cosmetologist. We will open a big clinic for you—Smiti's cosmetology and beauty clinic. No, no. What do you call it? Renew! How can I forget?'

And both of us giggled together.

Suddenly her mood changed. 'But you know one thing, when I went to the wards yesterday, I feel pity. There are so many women—not all are old, some are even in their late thirties and forties—suffering with advanced stages of cervical cancer, which is a 100 per cent preventable disease. When you take their history, none of them had gone for a Pap test.'

'Smiti, do you think this test works?'

'See, I will tell you. What we do in this test is that some cells are taken from the cervix of the lady with a long wooden ice-cream-spoon kind of thing. These cells are put in a glass slide, and the slide goes to the department of pathology for staining and examination under microscope. It's easy for a pathologist to detect if it has cancer cells or even those abnormal cells which have a chance to become cancer even ten years later.'

'Really? Are you saying ten years ahead, you can forecast if you will have cancer or not? That's so amazing. Amazing science!' I was thrilled.

'And you know, once this test was started at national level in some Western countries, in fifty years' time, it showed a fall of around 80 per cent in the incidence and deaths caused by cervical cancer.'

Smiti continued, 'George N. Papanicolaou was the man who changed the whole story. He was a doctor, but after some years of serving patients, he preferred research, like you. He did his PhD, and while he was studying menstrual cycle in guinea pigs, incidentally, he found some abnormal cells. Later, this became the basis of the famous Pap test, which transformed the entire history of cervical cancer.'

'Interesting.'

'And if you promise me that you will take me for a cold coffee, I will tell you one more interesting fact.'

'Okay, we will go for that, but whether I am going to pay for your coffee too, that I will decide after listening to your interesting thing.'

'Okay, boss, so here it is. This great scientist who changed the history of cervical cancer, Prof. George Papanicolaou, shares his birthday with my best friend.' She gave a flying kiss.

I jumped out of joy and hugged her. 'You are a sweetheart. Cold coffee with ice cream for you. Today I am gonna pay!'

<hr />

Everyone has slowly disappeared for work by then. Rene said, 'Finish it fast, Riya. I will wait for you. We have to do HPV typing of the positive samples today.'

I washed my coffee mug, wiped it dry, kept it in the overhead shelf, and went inside the lab.

When I was preparing the samples for the next test, Hybrid Capture, I got an idea. *Why don't I also get my sample tested sometime?*

Not a bad idea. I remember I had read somewhere that if the HPV test comes negative, its predictive value is so good that you don't need to do any test for cervical cancer for the next five years. You are safe!

I thought this was a good opportunity to take a self-sampling kit from Debora and do my own HPV. No one would even come to know. And after listening to Smiti's stories, I had no guts to go and get my Pap test done in India.

And it was decided. I took a self-sampling kit from Debora, saying that Anna was not able to come this time for her Pap test and she wanted me to get a kit for her. Debora handed me a kit without any suspicions or interrogations.

At home, I collected my sample, put it in my bag, and to took it to the lab.

On the next day, with the new batch of samples, I kept mine also and labelled it in sequence, CCS09-917.

Four hours later, it was nice to see your own DNA in a tiny plastic tube. I was in a hurry to process the samples today, so I kept it that day in the machine and set the PCR programme for the night.

I reached home. It was like any other normal day, but something exciting was going on inside me. Till today, I was testing samples of unknown women. It meant only marking negative as negative and running positive samples to know further which HPV strain was there. It was all so mechanical.

Today I did it for myself. The test suddenly had developed so much meaning. It was the DNA from my cells. I was feeling ticklish inside.

I wanted to share it with Raghav, but I knew he wouldn't take any interest. Neel? Yes, he will take all interest, but it was not something I could discuss with him. He was a friend or just an infatuation. *The more you go closer to him, it's gonna be more difficult for you, Riya*, I thought. *It's just a flirt. This relationship has a limited life of six months.*

Did I want it to be over?

'Infatuation is like marijuana, which gives you the best high yet gives you the worst headache ever.' I read it on a coffee shop somewhere.

◆───❖───◆

In the morning, I reached the lab before anyone else, took out all the forty DNA samples from the PCR machine, and started the gel electrophoresis. Once it was done, I went to the other room, where six computers with PCR-result-reading software were kept.

I placed the gel inside the reader with all the samples flanked by positive and negative controls on either side. I switched on the computer and opened the software. Forty lines in black and white appeared on the screen. The results looked weird. The last sample was not what it was expected to be. I closed the software, right-clicked the mouse to refresh, opened it again—same result. How was it possible?

Sample number CCS09-917 was supposed to be negative. I checked positive control once again. It was positive. Negative control was also negative. I couldn't understand what had gone wrong.

'Hi. Good morning.' Rene entered the computer lab. With the spinal reflex, I minimized the window as if I was watching porn. My face was pale, lips dry, and hands sweaty, I realized. As Rene left the lab, I restored the window again. It was the same. Something had gone wrong, grossly wrong.

I went to the main lab, opened the fridge, and took out the tray with the remaining DNA samples from yesterday's experiment. Unlike all other days when I prayed to God to let me not make any mistake, today I prayed to him, 'God, I hope it was a mistake in labelling the sample or arranging it.'

It was placed in the right place. I held the tube in my hand. The label read 917. Did I give a wrong number to my sample? I checked the list. All thirty-seven numbers matched in the tubes except this one. Positive and negative controls were properly labelled and were at their respective positions in the tray.

No, it can't be. Something has gone wrong, weirdly wrong. I will have to repeat the whole experiment.

———— ◆◈◆ ————

In the next two days, I was upset, busy repeating my experiment slowly and patiently, performing each step with utmost precaution.

This was the first time I had made excuses not to chat with Neel for three days in a row.

I sent a usual mail to Raghav. 'Everything is going on good here. How are you? How was your trip? Will Skype with you next Sunday. Busy this weekend with some experiments which have gone wrong and have to be repeated.'

The results were ready at 6 p.m. on Friday evening. I was the only one waiting in the lab, and the sample was positive!

I held my head with both hands. It was throbbing hard.

I poured in a glass of water and wiped my tears. Holding the same crumpled tissue tight in my fist, I ran down towards the back door. As I was reaching the lowest step, I saw a boy and a girl hugging and kissing each other intensely in a dark corner, unaware of my presence.

Two droplets rolled down my cheeks. 'People defy all norms, and nothing happens to them. What wrong did I do to get this bloody virus?'

Chapter 9

Retrospection

It was Saturday morning. I had dropped my plan to go to the lab today.

I didn't know what to do and with whom to share.

I called +3120-628-7232.

'Hi, Riya, what's up?' It was Debora on the other side.

'Debora, I am homesick. Would you mind if I come to your place today?'

'Why not! We are planning to take kids to Anne Frank House. You can join us.'

I kept silent.

'It's all up to you. I just said if you want to. What happened, Riya? Are you all right?' Her voice had a touch of worry.

'I am okay. But I need to talk to you.'

'Come over. I have enough and more time for you.'

———◆———

I took metro till Centrum and then the bus till Amsterdam Noord to reach Debora's house. I tried my best to look normal and behave normal despite the tsunami of questions killing me inside.

51

Debora has three children—Mic, Mac, and Noni (seven, five, and three years old). Her husband, Peter, has his own business of bikes. People say that in the Netherlands, there are more bicycles than residents. In cities like Amsterdam, up to 70 per cent of all journeys are made by bike. For the first time, I heard about something called biking culture. The history of revolutionary biking in the Netherlands is interesting. Before World War II, journeys here were predominantly made by bikes. During 1950 to 1960, car ownership rocketed in Europe. Paralleling other European countries, roads here also became increasingly congested. The bikers were squeezed to the kerb. This caused a huge rise in accidents and deaths on the roads. In the year 1971, estimated number of people killed in such motor accidents reached up to three thousand. Unfortunately, 450 of them were children. This led to a social movement demanding safer cycling conditions for children and was called Stop de Kindermoord (Stop the Child Murder). This name was derived from the headline of an article written by a journalist Vic Langenhoff, who had also lost his own child in one of such accidents. The Dutch government took this warning seriously and decided to invest in improved cycling infrastructure in the Netherlands.

As a result, now in Holland there is a vast network of cycling tract all around which is safer and very inviting. The tracks are wide and clearly marked. They have smooth surfaces and separate signs and lights, ensuring the safety of the bikers.

Peter had told me last time that people here prefer to invest more in bike locks than in the bikes.

'Why?' I was curious. I had never heard of locks for bicycles in India.

'Bike theft here is a more money-making business than designing, manufacturing, and selling the bikes,' he revealed the secret with a wink.

I had come to her house three times before this, so not only the kids but also the small Labrador named Snowy was familiar with me.

We had open-air Dutch lunch in the garden. Having finished lunch and while the kids were playing with Snowy, Debora asked, 'What happened, Riya? Is everything all right?'

I blinked my eyes. 'I don't know, but I want to tell you everything.'

'Go ahead then.'

'Not now. I will tell you in the night once you come back from the museum, and I don't want to come. Not feeling well today.'

She understood and didn't force me.

It was 7 p.m. when they returned. The kids were tired. We had dinner together, and they went to their respective rooms.

Peter also bid goodbye and left. I guess Debora had told him something. She took a bottle of wine and two glasses, and we sat in the backyard, only the two of us.

'Yeah, Riya. What's bothering you?'

'Actually . . .' And I told her the whole story with a feel of tremors in my voice.

'Oh, that's it, Riya? You know that HPV is a very common infection, and it will be present in around 80 per cent of those who are sexually active.'

'But how did I get it? That's the issue which is bothering me.'

'It comes through mucosal contact during sexual activity from one partner to another.'

'No, Debora, that's not the issue. Let me try to explain. I don't know whether you will understand.'

'Go ahead.'

'You see, I swear I never had a contact with anyone other than Raghav.' Now I could feel the moistness in my eyes.

'Who is doubting you, Riya? Maybe you got it from Raghav.'

'This is the thing which is bothering me. I know my hubby so well. He can't cheat on me. No!'

'Okay, cool down.' She held my hands and continued, 'You see, it's not about cheating on you. Maybe he had someone before he met you from where he had got this. This virus can remain in your body for years together without any signs or symptoms.'

'No, Debora. It doesn't happen like this in India, in our society. And I know Raghav is not that kind of a guy. If there was something, he would have shared it with me before we got married.' Tears rolled down my cheeks.

Debora thought probably that I was hurt and distressed with the test result, so she told me that it was late and I should go to bed. There was enough time to talk tomorrow.

I did what she said. I went to the bed but couldn't sleep. Depressing, agonizing, psychotic thoughts were filling my mind. Suddenly my mind said, *Maybe this is God's way of punishing me for what I was doing these days, which I had named 'Just a flirt!'*

I don't know when I fell asleep, but when I got up, oh no, it was ten o'clock. I took a shower, got ready, and climbed down the stairs. I saw the kids were finishing their breakfast while Peter and Debora had decided to wait for me.

Following breakfast, Peter left home with the three kids and Snowy. It looked like a pre-planned arrangement. Now there were only me, Debora, and the silence.

She went near the side table and got me some small booklets and papers. Debora said, 'You read these for more information on HPV and its spread.'

I took all the papers, and she continued, 'I thought about it in the night. I feel now that rather than finding out how it happened, we should focus on your health now. Forget about the blame game. Process your sample tomorrow for HPV typing. It's a good opportunity because I am not sure whether you will be able to get all this done in India. Keep it with the other samples like you have done earlier. Don't tell it to anyone else. I am here for you.' She was holding my hands and was sitting on the floor, directly looking in my eyes.

I forgot that I was in a foreign country. I felt as if I was there with my mom, my sister, or my best friend. Or perhaps Debora was an angel, having all those three within her.

Chapter 10

Best Friends

'I want to give you news, a real good one. Call me ASAP.' This was the message from Smiti.

I know her. I thought it must be about a proposal or an engagement, or had she fixed a wedding date without asking me?

'I don't have a personal phone number here. Come for Skype in the evening (10–11 p.m., Indian time). I will be waiting. Any change of time, please message.'

I messaged and ran towards the station. I was already a bit late.

The whole day I kept on guessing. *Is it Amit? Or Dilip? Or is it someone new?*

Smiti is a fun-loving and very straightforward girl. She had crush on a different guy every month. She once said, 'Riya, it's not a matter of choice. We have to change our crushes with changing clinical posting in medical school. Otherwise, we don't have the zeal to go to that ward every morning.'

'So how many inspirations like this do you have till now?'

'I don't keep a count, darling. They come, and they go. It's as simple as that.'

'Really?'

'But don't take it seriously. It's just a timepass, nothing to hurt anybody and get involved.'

'So cool you are.'

Today I was in a real rush to finish my work. I took permission from Debora to leave at four thirty to five as soon as my lab work was done.

We had a meeting today from 5 to 6 p.m. with a guest from Maastricht University, but the professor was supposed to deliver his lecture in Dutch, so it didn't make sense for me to stay back.

It was 10 p.m. in my laptop (Indian time), and I was in front of the laptop. I opened Skype and was ready from my side. Within ten minutes, Smiti came online with a big smile.

'Any guess?' she asked.

'You are getting married.'

'Wow. You are almost there, but I am not going to marry without you being here with me.'

'Engagement?' I asked.

'Yep.' She blushed.

'But who is the guy? You decided without asking me?' I made a bad face.

'You know him very well.'

'I know so many names.' I continued to show her that I was angry.

'You have met him, darling. Now please cheer up. Otherwise, I will call him now and say no to him.'

Suddenly my brain got alerted, and by the time she finished her sentence, my brain recalled the past, and I shouted, 'Sameer Chaddha?'

She smiled. 'Correct.'

'Are you sure you are saying this?'

'Yeah, Riya. I thought about it a lot. I wanted someone whom I really knew well and someone who knows me the way I am. Chaddha is my group mate from first year.'

'Hmm . . . I know.'

'And moreover, he is a fun-loving guy. With all due respect to you and Raghav, sometimes I wonder what you guys do when you two are all alone. Raghav hardly speaks, and you also stop speaking in front of him.' She winked.

'I need not tell you what we do when we are alone.' I was in a good mood for a change.

'I am a doctor. I know everything.'

'But he didn't do his postgrad from the same institute. You said he had gone back to Delhi.' I changed the topic, and I wanted to know more about them rather than discussing my own fucked life.

'Yes, you are right. He joined general surgery in Maulana Azad Medical College. He is now doing MCh in plastic surgery from there.'

'Oh really? Cool.'

'You see, plastic surgery and dermatology will be a superb combination.'

'Oh yeah, that didn't come to me. You are a clever girl, I knew. But my friend is so calculative, I didn't know.' I smiled.

'I have one more blasting secret. Should I tell you?'

'Yeah, please, go ahead. I have put on my seat belt.'

'They already own a clinic in NCR. We will just have to expand and modernize it. No tension.'

'Wow, so much of planning. I am proud of you.'

'So the engagement is fixed on 30 May. I am sad that you won't be there, but the wedding is going to be next year.'

'Good. We will do all the shopping and preparations together.'

'Yeah, and I forgot to tell you, from next month, I will be in Pune for six months. You let me know when you are going to Mumbai so I will also come over for a weekend. So many things to talk about.'

'For sure. I also miss talking to you so much.'

'See you then. Bye-bye.'

'Goodnight, and all the best for your new life.'

'Hi.' I had a new topic to discuss with Neel today.

'Hey, girl. You made me wait so much today,' Neel said.

'Sorry. I was talking to Smiti, my best friend. She is getting married to Sameer Chaddha.' And the story followed.

He kept on listening to me, showing equal interest. I don't know whether he was really enjoying or not, but I enjoyed sharing it with him. I told him about our childhood and our dreams. Then I asked, 'Hey, what did you actually want to do in your life?'

'Me?'

'Yeah, obviously you. There is no third person here.'

'Are you sure you are interested in knowing that?'

'Of course. But don't tell me that the life you are living now is actually what you dreamt of—to become a boring engineer and work for a bossy boss day and night.'

'No, never. My dream is to open a chain of resorts all around the world some day.'

'Oh really! That's so interesting.'

'I want to save enough money to invest in the first one. I have big plans to follow.'

'Wow, impressed.'

'I should at least earn that much money so that the banks don't deny giving loans to me.'

'Ha ha . . . that's true. Have you thought of a name?'

'Not actually. You have some suggestions?'

'And what about the food? Continental, Indian, or Chinese? Oh, I am sorry, it's not a restaurant. Yours is a resort, so there will be various restaurants for all kinds of food, I guess.'

'Nope. On this I am very clear, only Indian food. That too pure vegetarian.'

'Ha ha ha . . . Then forget it. Nobody will go to your resort, Mr Neel Agarwal.'

'You also, Riya?' he asked, making a cute baby face.

'Even if nobody goes to your resort, tell me once when you have done it. I will definitely go there before I die. It's a promise.'

'You are a real friend, my best friend.' He seemed so proud.

Chapter 11

Peace of Mind

I felt a bit placid now, having spoken my heart out to Debora. My mind was also diverted by the newly added chapter in Smiti's life. I spoke to Raghav, my parents, and my in-laws, as was the routine on Sundays. The only connection I had with Neel was the Internet, so I sent him just a small message: 'Very busy. Don't think I will get time this week too. Take care!'

I had gone through the literature and had searched also in Google as suggested by Debora. Though the more I read, the more confused I got.

I realized that the HPV is quite complex. They mentioned there are more than two hundred types of this virus. It is one of the most contagious infective agents, but it can come only through intimate contact. Anyone who is sexually active can get HPV. HPV is so common that around 70–80 per cent of sexually active men and women get it at some point in their lives. Usually, HPV infection has no signs and symptoms, so it is practically impossible to guess that someone has got the infection until the test reveals so. Most people don't even know that they are harbouring HPV inside.

Then I came across a line, saying, 'You can get HPV even if you have had sex with only one person.' I flipped of the page which read, 'If your sex partner has had many partners, you can develop symptoms years after you have sex with someone who is infected, making it hard to know when you first became infected or from where the infection actually came.'

I kept that booklet aside. This was complex.

Another pamphlet with a picture of a girl and boy laughing together at something said:

You can do several things to lower your chances of getting HPV:

1. Get vaccinated. HPV vaccines are safe and effective. HPV vaccines are given in three shots over six months.
2. Get screened for cervical cancer and routine screening with Pap test.
3. Use condoms every time you have sex. This can lower your chances of getting HPV.
4. Be in a mutually monogamous relationship. That means having sex only with someone who only has sex with you.

I learnt that there is no treatment for the virus itself. However, there are treatments for the health problems that HPV can cause like warts, premalignant lesions, and cancer.

Debora's words were echoing in my ears. 'I should now think about myself. What should be done now?' I remembered I had gone to meet Smiti to take advice on contraception a few days prior to my wedding. With that, she had told me something about some HPV vaccine, which women should take before their sexual debut. However, since it was still at an experimental stage, we had not discussed much about it.

It has been now around more than five years. It must have come to the market for use, I thought. I opened Google to search, and I was right. Two companies, GlaxoSmithKline and Merck, have launched their HPV vaccine with the names Cervarix and Gardasil. Thank God there was some hope now.

But still, there were a lot of questions I wanted to get the answers for.

———◆———

On the next day at my workplace, I met Debora and told her about what I was thinking.

Debora replied, 'Group D5, headed by Professor Berkhof, is involved in Cervarix vaccine trial here. But as far as I know, this vaccine has to be used before you get the infection.'

'But I read that it is given to girls without any screening. Then how do you know that they are not infected?'

'You are right, Riya. But you know it is given at a very young age before their sexual debut, so there is no chance that they will have the virus, as HPV can come only and only through sexual contact.'

'Hmm.' She had a point.

While I was engrossed in my web of analysing, she said, 'But I got an idea. I think it makes sense.'

I interrupted, 'What?'

'You see, we are going to do HPV typing of your sample today. Mostly, I guess it will have those strains which are not that harmful. If it is not positive for the strains which are in the vaccine, the most dreaded ones, type 16 or type 18, you can still take the vaccine for your protection and prevention. Since you don't know how you got it, there is no way we can say that by doing this or not doing this, further infections can be prevented.'

'It's too complex, Debora. My mind has stopped working. Please tell me whatever you feel is right. I will do it. Once I go back to India, things will become more difficult for me. I want to get rid of this problem here.' I was upset.

As per Debora's instruction, I started Hybrid Capture 2 for the thirty-three samples which had come positive for HPV, including mine.

Hybrid Capture 2, also known as HC2, is a test that can detect many high-risk HPV types. I was reading through the whole information brochure. Now these tests, which were only a project till the last week, had become personally important to me. I prayed to the God and kept my fingers crossed.

I never thought this tiny microscopic creature which measures just around fifty nanometre, with only eight thousand base pairs (compared to human DNA, which has three billion base pairs), would one day snatch away my peace of mind and jumble up my life like this.

Chapter 12

What's Wrong, What's Right?

Debora and I and the Hybrid Capture 2 results were in front of us. Both of us were silent. There was nothing to talk about. Sample number CCS09-917 was positive for HPV 16.

There was nothing to confabulate, nothing to discuss. This result straight away required a Pap test and probably a tissue biopsy for conformation to know if this high-risk HPV strain had really started the interplay at the level of my tissues. Pap smear, unlike HPV, was not a good option to be done while in Holland, as it meant taking an appointment with a gynaecologist, taking a smear, and sending it to the pathology lab for staining and microscopic examination.

I went to meet Professor Bart, who was the head of the histology section of VU University. He was a very helpful person, and I had met him while working in the histology department in the month of February to get some known positive and negative samples directly from the paraffin blocks. However, it seemed impossible to get the test done without going through the proper channels.

Tired mentally more than physically, I requested Debora to take me out somewhere where I can fetch some peace my mind. She suggested some coffee shop at the Centrum, but it was too much for me to choose. So finally, we settled for a descent bar near her house.

Till now, friends here had failed to impress me with hundreds of qualities and feeling of moderate alcohol consumption. But today was different. I wanted to drink. Drink till I forget everything. Debora readily agreed to accompany me, as she knew my zero skills and experience at drinking. She was worried about me and my safety, I guess.

Debora proposed I first take a glass of rosé wine. I agreed. We sat at a corner. We didn't say anything to each other. When I finished the first glass, my whole body felt warm and cosy. I ordered now for Robert Mondavi's Woodbridge, the longest name in the menu. I was slowly getting out.

After a few more glasses (I don't remember the count), I started feeling like I was one giant vibrating being. Music was sounding more relaxing; surrounding people were more attractive and happy. I forgot all the pains and strains of life. Life looked beautiful.

The next moment, I felt like crying, crying aloud. 'I am a good girl. I never did anything wrong.'

Debora smiled. Probably she knew it was not me but the alcohol inside me that was speaking out. Now tears were rolling down continuously.

'I wanted Dad and Mom to decide. And this is what they decided for me, Raghav—good boy, good business, and good family. They said I will be happy throughout my life. Debora, you tell me, do I look happy?'

'Don't be sad. It happens.' Debora tried to console me.

I got agitated. 'What? What happens? Does everyone gift their wives this? Husbands gift rings, flowers, and love to their wives. And what did my husband give me? Yeah, something different, something extraordinary. He gave me HPV.' I kept my head on the table and kept on sobbing.

'Okay, Riya, cool down now.'

'No, Debo, it's my mistake. Dad said, "You decide." I decided, but I decided wrong. My mistake, it's entirely my mistake. He never loved me. He never bothered what I wanted.'

'What you wanted?'

'I wanted every moment to be full of love and happiness. I wanted to laugh with him. I wanted to cry with him. I wanted to share small, little moments of happiness with him—nothing big. I wanted to listen to his problems, and I wanted him to listen to me.'

'Everything will be good once you go back. You talk to him.'

'No. I don't want to talk to anybody. I have messed up my life.' I started crying again. I was getting little out of control now. Debora decided that we must leave now. She dropped me up till my door to ensure that I reached home safely.

I opened the door. I was tired, lazy but not sleepy. I opened my laptop. The first thing I noticed was the bright-green dot indicating that Neel was online.

I wrote, 'Flirting with another chick?'

'No, waiting for you. Have been doing the same thing all the evening for the last four days. How busy this work has made you! Hope you are planning to return. I feel if you work like this, Dutch government will capture such a hard-working girl for their benefit.'

I couldn't understand, not because what he said was long and complicated but because I was under the effect of various wines, so I said, 'Maybe. I don't know.'

Neel got some doubt. 'Riya, it has been so many days since I have spoken to you. Please come on Skype.'

'I am tired.'

'Please for ten minutes, please. I promise I won't take much time.'

Whether I agreed or I couldn't resist, I don't remember. Anyways, it's one or the same.

I opened Skype and saw my picture there. My curly hair was shabby. My face was more pink than usual. I removed my muffler on seeing it in the picture. I had forgotten to remove it, I guess.

'You look pretty. Doesn't look like you came straight from work.' He winked.

'I will tell you. I will tell you everything. But you have to promise you won't judge me.'

'Promise, Dr Riya Goyal, I won't judge you for anything in my whole lifetime.'

He could always bring a smile to me. 'You know, Neel, I am drunk. My test is positive.'

'Hey, girl, what are you talking about? You should not drink when you are pregnant. That's the only thing I know about pregnancy.'

'Ha ha ha ha ha ha ha ha ha . . . I am not pregnant. It's not about pregnancy test. Leave it. You won't understand.' I felt like rolling down. After few seconds, my head touched the table, and I was asleep.

I don't know whether it was minutes or hours, but when I woke up, suddenly I saw Neel was still there, staring at me. 'I was wondering if anyone can look so beautiful even when she is asleep.'

'I am sleepy. I want to go to bed. Will talk to you tomorrow.' I felt embarrassed. I closed my laptop lid and slid inside the quilt.

I saw something beautiful when I opened my MacBook next morning.

> If she is amazing, she won't be easy.
> If she is easy, she won't be amazing.
> If she is worth it, you won't give up.
> If you give up, you are not worthy . . .
> Truth is everybody is going to hurt you:
> You just gotta find the one worth suffering for!
>
> (Bob Marley)

And I have found her. I am sure.

Chapter 13

Planning and Planning

I was feeling fresh, light, and dreamy. I don't know whether it was the effect of alcohol last night or Bob Marley's words.

I had decided yesterday with Debora that I was not going to think about this HPV diagnosis, as I had only a month left here. I had to compile all my work and make a report. It had to be submitted on time. Moreover, there was no further testing which could be done here, so I had a long list of things which I wanted to do once I reach India.

I had already changed my tickets to Amsterdam–New Delhi now after telling Raghav that I was missing Mom and Dad a lot. Plan was to meet them at my sister's place in Delhi. I planned to stay there for two days. After that, I wanted to go to Kanpur to spend some days with my in-laws. Raghav was very happy with the plan and readily agreed. It was not just meeting my in-laws. Something else was going on in my mind. I wanted to know Raghav's past in case there was something.

Next, I wanted from there to go straight to Mumbai. No, there were no plans to meet Neel, as we had promised each other. But I wanted to meet Smiti, who was doing some training in laser these days in Pune. She had agreed to come to Mumbai for a few days in the month of August. I had not told her anything yet. However, I wanted to discuss it with her. We shared all our secrets and fantasies since we were small girls. Moreover, before going to any gynaecologist, I wanted her opinion. It mattered the most to me when it came to something in the medical field.

Rene entered the room when I was scribbling the to-do list in my notepad.

'I am in,' she said with excitement. 'Riya, what's in the menu?'

'Not yet decided, Rene, but everything is going to be Indian.'

'Hope it won't be spicy,' Susan joined in.

The discussion was about the Indian night which we had planned during the last weekend of my stay here. The date and venue were not finalized yet. With all the present probabilities, it was going to be Debora's house. We had planned to invite all those who were involved in my project (directly or indirectly).

That day last year when Raghav got angry with me for my poor cooking skills, I resolved to learn cooking. I joined a cookery class secretly, which was at a walking distance from my home in Mumbai. Every afternoon, I went there for eight weeks and learned a lot of Indian, Chinese, and Continental cuisines. As I had no other work other than to write proposal and prepare some papers to apply for the fellowship on those days, I planned to use my time in the skill which I was lacking. I had realized that the way to a man's heart is through his stomach. Though I was very upset with Raghav's attitude that day, I still loved him. I wanted to learn to cooking for the sake of my love.

'Can I bring my boyfriend too for the Indian party?' Susan asked.

'Why not? He is most welcome.'

'He happens to be half Indian. His mom is Dutch but his dad is an Indian. He always loves to go to Indian restaurants,' Susan detailed.

'He can bring his dad too, Susan. I am sure he will definitely enjoy as I want to give that night a perfect Indian touch. I call it *Indiase Nacht in Holland.*'

The time was moving fast-forward, and we had already reached middle of the month. With all my speed, I was compiling my work and was busy preparing the report.

Sideways, the plans for the much-awaited night were at its ascendency. The date was fixed for 27 June (Saturday). The venue was the much-expected Amsterdam Noord, Debora's house. The menu had starters, main course, and the dessert. Everything was Indian, purely Indian. We had roamed around almost all Indian, Pakistani, and Turkish stores to find the best possible ingredients.

It was not only about the food. We had Indian music from *Jagjeet Singh Ghajals* to old melodies and latest Bollywood hits. On one of the walls, we had set the projector screen where a Bollywood movie *Jodha Akbar*, starring Aishwarya Rai and Hrithik Roshan, was being played with volume set at mute. Still, the attention of men was fixed whenever Aishwarya came on the screen. We all girls were smiling at the sight, our eyes telling each other, *Men will be men.*

I was dressed like a perfect Indian girl. When I came out of my room in my full Indian get-up, Debora, Susan,

Elsa, Rene, and all the girls started shouting, 'We also want the black punct.'

I turned into the room and came back with a packet of bindis. Everyone wanted one. And trust me, those black puncts looked even better on those spotless white foreheads.

We clicked pictures, danced, had food, clicked more picture, played games, and were dead tired. Professor Harrington got up to say something.

'Dear Riya, in six months you have become not only a friend, a colleague, but a part of our family—the CCA family. With your warm and welcoming smile, you have gained so many friends in a foreign land. I am proud to say it's not only about individual bonds. Your Indian gestures have brought even all of us much closer to each other in the past six months.

'Not only socially, I feel all of you agree with me that Riya has been a great asset to our research team too. Your hard work is worth appreciating. I don't know whether it's Indian luck or your stars that out of the ten random genes I gave you to work on, three have come out with significant positive results. And two, as all of you have seen during her presentation, are giving predictive values above 90 per cent. Debora and I have seen the real struggle. We choose some 200 probable genes two years ago, which might be methylated in HPV-infected cervical cancer tissues. In two years' time, out of some 130 genes, we could find only 6 good markers. And here is this girl. Can you compare?'

Friends clapped.

He continued, 'We are planning to patent these markers in the future once we are finished with all the probable genes. And if it works, you will be the one who discovered the two markers in the diagnostic panel.'

I looked straight towards Debora. She was already staring at me. Our silent eyes met and said, *Not only this, we have discovered something more—something not that great to feel about, something which mattered only to me, something which was a secret, something which had changed my opinion, my dreams about my past, present, and future.*

It was 28 June, last day of our six months of friendship.

I terribly want her to come here, as she is miles away,
What's far, what's near? That is the question of the day.
Neither friendship nor love, we share a zone of grey;
You won't find this affection anywhere you may survey.
Will always be there for you, despite prospects roll or sway,
You can trust me any day in every way,
wanna let you know today.

Neel and I were on Skype, saying goodbyes, as we had promised that we were never going to meet in real life.

I told him, 'Thank you for everything—for making me laugh when I was sad, for tolerating me when I was grumpy, for understanding me when I was moody. Thanks for everything, Neel.'

'Anything else, madam?'

I laughed. 'You are never serious. You will never understand what you mean to me.'

'Okay. For that, can I ask you something? Only once, please.'

I was puritanical. 'No.'

'Only once. I want to see you, to meet you. I will never bother you again, I promise.'

Though it was getting difficult for me too, I kept my sternness upright. 'This is the time to keep your first promise that we will never meet in real life. You are not allowed to break that and make a new one.'

'Okay.' He made a sad face.

'I want to feel proud of this friendship and cherish the beautiful moments till the end of my life. I want to remember you as a man of your word. Please.'

He didn't say anything, just smiled. For the first time, I could see his eyes were also getting moist. And then he wrote, 'How lucky I am to have someone who makes saying goodbye so hard.' And he logged off. I froze in front of my MacBook for some time and then wiped my tears, got up, and started packing my stuff.

PART II

PART II

Chapter 14

To Be Ignored or Not?

Once upon a time known as the Manchester of India, Kanpur, nestling in the bank of the river Ganga, is one of the main industrial cities in north India. I received a very warm welcome from my in-laws when I reached Kanpur.

On my way back from Amsterdam, I had stayed for two days at my sister's place at Delhi, where my mom and dad had also come. Mom had worked during the summer break this year so that she could take leave during July and August. Mom recently was promoted as the vice principal of the high school where she had been working for almost thirty-eight years now. Didi was expecting her second baby sometime in mid August, so the leave was planned in such a way that they can meet me too. Dad was supposed to go back to join work at his office in a week's time. Mom would stay here till didi's delivery, so I held a very good chance to meet her once more when I went back to Mumbai via Delhi.

This was the first time I had come to stay with my in-laws in the last four and a half years since our marriage. Raghav and I used to come here together, mostly during festivals or at times during some extended weekends, more of less like guests. So practically, this was my first time to stay like a family member here and discern *Maa* and *Baba* more intimately.

Maa said, 'I am so happy, Riya, that you made this programme. Once you join a job, then it becomes so tough to get leaves, isn't it?'

'Yeah, Maa, that's the reason. First time I am having a feeling that it's my home.'

'Why not, *beta*. Everything is yours. I suggested Raghav also that both of you should plan to stay with us now. We are getting old, you see,' Baba said when we were having a relaxed dinner.

'You please understand, Goyal Jee, he told you he can't operate his business from Kanpur. His main offices are in Mumbai, Delhi, and Bangalore,' Maa interrupted him.

'Neera, you know only one thing—how to fight. Let me continue. We can stay in Delhi with them. We have a house there also, and we have so many relatives in Delhi.'

'I am not going to leave this house. This is not just a house. This is a palace of dreams for me. I have a connection with everything here. These roses on the pots, the grass in the garden, peacocks that come to the roof during monsoon, the flow of Ganga behind—I get my life from them. I can't leave this.' Maa was getting emotional. I caressed her shoulder with my left hand.

Baba changed the topic. 'So what's the plan for tomorrow, Riya?'

'Baba, you suggest.'

'Okay, I will give you options. We can go to JK Temple and Moti Jheel or to the zoo. We may even go to Bithoor if you like.'

Maa stopped him. 'Riya, it's really sunny and humid to go out these days. I suggest let Baba go to work. *Saas* and *Bahu* will stay back. I will show you my secret museum.'

Shocked, I asked, 'Where is this secret museum?'

'It's in the basement. Wait till the morning.'

Maa and Baba looked at each other and smiled.

We bid goodnight to each other, and I went to my room. I meant our room. This was the room where I had spent my first night of a new life exactly four and a half years ago. Lying on the bed, I saw the roof. It looked like the colours have changed. It was pale and grey now. That day it looked so glittery, so colourful, and so much full of life. Or did the background had the same grey colour that day too, but with the temporary decor, I failed to see the reality?

———◆———

I was ready next morning. Maa had made *poha* for breakfast. She was still in the kitchen with beads of sweat hanging on her forehead. Baba was sitting on the sofa, reading newspaper. Without noticing me, he shouted, 'Neera! How much time do you take to make a cup of tea?'

I went straight inside the kitchen, poured tea in a tumbler, kept it in a tray, and stood in front of Baba, who was still lost on the layers of his newspaper.

'Keep it down,' he said. When he noticed the next moment that it was not Maa but me, he folded his newspaper and kept it aside.

'Sit here, beta. Did you sleep well? Hope you didn't get scared alone upstairs.'

'No, Baba, not at all. I will go and help Maa, so that we all can chat together during breakfast.'

I started arranging the table as Maa was busy giving the final touch to the breakfast. In my mind, subconsciously I started comparing. I had seen my mother working as a teacher since I was very small, and Dad used to really help Mom a lot. It was not fifty-fifty. I will say it was sixty-forty, with my dad being on the 'sixty' side. They laughed, and they teased each other while doing household chores all the time. If Mom was cooking, Dad would chop all the vegetables, make the dough, and arrange the table. Then together, they would wash the dishes and clean the kitchen.

On one hand, my mother-in-law was a homemaker, so it was taken for granted that all work related to home was her duty. On the other hand, home for Baba meant only sitting and relaxing. He was an electrical engineer from BITS Pilani. After a few years, he thought of starting his own company, which was something related to initial electrical work set-up for office buildings. He still was continuing to do the same with some thirty employees under him. Though he had a hectic schedule, his lifestyle was more or less sedentary. As a result, he had already developed diabetes and a big paunch.

We all settled down for breakfast.

'Tasty poha, Maa. Please give me the recipe.'

'Riya, I just learnt it with trial and error. You have done a certified course. You should be the one teaching me.'

Baba said, 'Yeah, Riya, teach her some new things. I am bored of eating the same stuff for years together now.'

Maa's face fell. 'Baba, you should appreciate that Maa is cooking every day, three times a day, for you. Raghav always says, "Whatever is normal, actually that's the luxury." When you see other families, you will realize what Maa does for you.' I didn't intend to make it serious, so I continued, 'And,

Baba, how is your sugar these days? This paunch is not good for diabetics, they say.'

'Fasting blood sugar was 168 last week. He doesn't listen to me at all. He ate so many mangoes this season despite my repeated warnings,' Maa informed me.

'Don't worry, tomorrow onwards, Baba and I are going for jogging at five in the morning. I am going to fix an appointment with the doctor for the evening today. I want to meet a dietician also. Baba, be ready!' All of us laughed together.

I cleaned the table and helped Maa to wash the dishes and clean her kitchen.

Then I reminded her, 'Maa what about the secret museum?'

We two were in the basement.

Maa opened a huge black iron box with patches of rust on its surface. She took out a bag from there and kept it on the side table. One more bag and one more bag followed. She kept the lid of the box down to close it and told me to pull a chair and sit. She also sat down on a stool. By the time I got the chair after dusting it, she had already spread something on the table. There were two small green-and-cream school uniforms spread neatly on the table. I went close to see them. There were some cross-stitched letters on the upper left corners of the two sweaters. One read 'Raghav', and the other 'Vartika'. I was amazed.

She rubbed her hand on those two words and said, 'These are my gems. I have given one to you. Take care of him.'

I hugged her.

'Do you want to see more?' she asked.

I said, 'Yes. I am excited.' She handed me a bundle of notebooks. All were covered nicely with bamboo sheets and with a thin layer of transparent plastic over that. The label read:

Raghav Goyal
Roll Number: 19
Class: LKG
School: Little Millennium, Kanpur

I was thrilled to read it. I couldn't imagine six-foot-and-an-inch-tall Raghav wearing a tiny school uniform with a bow tie and going to LKG. Ha ha ha . . . How cute!

There were more surprises inside. There were three fruits on the first page of the art book: an apple, a banana, and a mango. Apple was red, banana was yellow, and the mango was black. I couldn't control laughing. I asked, 'Maa which mango is black? It is a rotten one!'

'You know, Riya, Baba had asked him the same question. He was three and a half years old. He replied, "It is an African mango. Baba, you have not gone to Africa, so you don't know." Baba couldn't answer anything.'

In his maths book, he seemed to be in such a hurry to answer that some answers were given before the equals sign or some seemed riding the equals sign. I knew mathematics was his favourite subject, and today I got to see the evidence too.

We kept seeing the precious articles in Maa's secret museum and didn't realize it was already two, and we had not done any preparation for lunch. Maa saw the clock on the wall, and before she could throw a fit, I kept everything inside, locked the box, and dragged her upstairs.

It was fun cooking together. By the time Baba reached home, lunch was ready though a light one. Anyways, it matched the sort of food that a diabetic should eat, so we were ready with our explanation: 'It was not a delay. It was a dedication to Baba's diabetes.' I smiled at Maa.

I developed a really strong bond with Maa. We spoke for hours and hours together. She told me about our family, about other relatives, about Raghav's childhood days, about Raghav–Vartika fights.

We were looking through old albums, starting from Maa and Baba's wedding album. We had reached now when Raghav was born. Each picture looked like a beautiful moment well captured and preserved. Maa had a story or at least a punchline for most of the pics.

'This was during his playschool. He was such a crybaby.'

'This was Vartika's birthday—third, I think. After the party, both had a fight. Raghav fell down from the bed and got his hand fractured.'

Baba also joined us. We finished looking through some more albums.

I made ginger tea. Sipping the tea, we were looking through the albums. Pictures were so many, but there were more stories with each of those.

Raghav looked like a very chubby and naughty boy in his childhood as compared to the serious Raghav I had seen. It was thrilling to see him metamorphosing from a fat tiny baby to a thin and sober teenager to a handsome tall adult.

Then there was this pic, and I stopped. 'Maa who is she?'

There was silence for a few seconds, and then Baba replied, 'She is Raghav's colleague. I don't remember her name.'

We turned pages. I noticed that Raghav didn't seem to have many friends, but this one girl could be traced in many pictures. If I had seen this album a year ago, I wouldn't have bothered much, but now, something was definitely bothering me.

She was a very pretty and tall girl. She looked like a foreigner but difficult to say confidently, as she had an Indian glimpse also.

I spotted her again in the next photo and asked, 'Maa, is she a foreigner?'

'Yes, Riya. She was a Russian. She worked in India for some years in Raghav's company, and I think she has gone back to Russia now.'

'Oh, I see.' I picked up the next album.

'Now my eyes are tired. If you don't mind, we will see the rest tomorrow,' Maa said.

'Anyways, now most of these are after you came to our family. We will look at them some other time. I am tired too.' I felt they didn't want me to see more of it. Was I getting too direct?

Each new day came with a new agenda. I tried searching Raghav's room in a hope that I might find some hint, a diary, some card, or any clue, but I failed. I tried to speak to Maa but she seemed to be more faithful to her son. Whenever

I tried to create such plot of discussion, she intellectually changed the topic.

Then I thought of an idea. I thought of talking to Vartika. I called her and gave her an idea if she could come home this weekend because I was leaving the next weekend. She readily agreed to my proposal.

Vartika is a really lovely girl. She is ten years younger to Raghav, and in no time we two became best buddies. We shared our stories, jokes, secrets, and adventures. On Sunday night after Baba and Maa had gone off to sleep and we were still busy chatting on the rooftop, I said, 'Vartika, if you don't mind, can I ask you something?'

'Why not, *bhabhi*, go ahead. Anything for you.'

'Was there someone else in Raghav's life before I came?'

There was silence, dead silence. Far-off moving truck on the roads became more obvious for a minute or two. It looked like Vartika was trying to organize her answer. She asked, 'Are you sure you want to know the story?'

'Yeah, very sure. Please tell me. I won't tell it to anyone. This will remain a secret between you and me.'

'There was a girl, and bhaiya really liked her a lot. She is a Russian, married and separated. Raghav bhaiya wanted to marry her and no one else, but Maa and Baba didn't allow this. Baba said he will hang himself if he did so. Maa threatened him that he has to marry someone because, otherwise, what will the society say? When he resisted, Maa said, "Okay, I will eat poison, then do whatever you wish to do."'

'Oh, but Raghav didn't tell me anything about this.'

'You know him, bhabhi, he doesn't talk much to anyone. I so desperately wanted to talk to him before your wedding. I tried also . . .'

'About what?' I interrupted.

'Bhaiya is not going to give up, I knew. They really like each other a lot. I wanted to tell him, "Don't spoil the life of that innocent new girl coming into your life.'"

'What? What do you mean?'

'Bhabhi, I feel they are still together.'

I was shocked, too shocked to continue the discussion.

I asked, 'What's her name?'

'Sara. Sara Antonovich.'

I couldn't sleep the whole night. All the blocks of puzzle were fitting into place now.

So this was the Russian girl who had got the virus from her ex-husband or from God-knows-where. That's why I was the only lucky/unlucky girl Raghav agreed to marry without much thinking. That's why he didn't need me. It didn't matter whether I was there or not, whether I was talking to him or not because that bitch was there to talk to him, to give him company. I cried and cried and cried the whole night.

But why does this name Sara sound familiar to me? Raghav never told me about her. Oh, now I remember . . . the unanswered phone call on our wedding night. The mobile screen flashed in front of my eyes—'Sara calling'.

Chapter 15

Not Fair

She didn't look nice; she looked like art, and art isn't
supposed to look nice; it is supposed to make you feel
something . . . And you made me feel miraculous!

It had been a month or a little more than a month since I
had come back to India. After having spent a good one
month in the spy world, having unfolded some painfully
mysterious facts, today I landed in Mumbai.

I had not said anything to Raghav about my secret
missions or what triggered me to take up this mission,
although he might have already known from the sources
where I had tried to extract all the information. He had
come to pick me up at the airport. I could say with surety
that we behaved exactly the same as we used to behave
earlier.

'Hi,' he said and gave me a hug.

It was the same Dolce & Gabbana smell, but the feeling
was so different now.

We spoke about all the general things on the way to
home.

He opened the door, and wow, what an amazing feeling.
It was my house. It was exactly the same as I had left it seven

months ago. Though there was so much transformation inside my heart for my feeling towards Raghav, my home gave me the same comfort as it used to. I sat on the couch. He sat next to me and wrapped his right arm around me. 'Your home missed you!'

'And what about my hubby?' I asked, looking straight in his eyes.

He smiled, withdrew his arm slowly and, switching on the television with the remote, said, 'Obviously, me too.'

I sensed my rudeness and decided to remain cool till I find a proper moment to talk to him directly.

I had heard of families and relationships shatter because of misunderstandings and accusations. So I was sure I was not going to believe anything till Raghav confessed it. And even after that, I thought every human being deserved a second chance. Mistake is a single page in the story of life. But relationship is like a book with all stories together. We don't lose a full book for a single page. Plausibly, I still loved him somewhere deep within. Our relationship looked wrapped and lost in a layer of dust, but I still felt I could clean the dust of doubts and misunderstandings and return it in its much required gleaming shine. I was trying to accommodate the word Sara in the book of our life, but the condition was that it should remain as a past, forgotten chapter.

I went to the kitchen, searching something to eat, and I found that Sunita (my maid) had not forgotten to keep a thermos flask full of ginger tea with two empty cups in a tray, like she used to do before. I opened the fridge, and there were my favourite muffins. I got everything to the table and called Raghav, who was busy smoking in the balcony.

We talked. I was feeling better.

'Oh shit, look at me, I forgot to call Mom and Dad that I had reached safely.'

'I had messaged them that you are in safe hands.' He smiled.

'But still.' I took my mobile out from my bag and switched it on. A message flashed: 'Airtel network welcomes you in Mumbai.' And then there was another one: 'She didn't look nice. She looked like art, and art isn't supposed to look nice; it is supposed to make you feel something . . . and you made me feel miraculous!'

Who's this? Unknown number. I was talking to myself. I went inside the bathroom with my towel, clothes, and phone. I read it again, '+91-9449619260.' This was not a familiar number. I saw the time. It said ten minutes past two. My flight landed around one thirty. I was out of the airport by two, I guess. *Who is this?* My heart had a few doubts, but my mind was not hearing that voice. I pasted the number in Truecaller. Truecaller searched it for a while and gave me the answer: 'Neel Agrawal, Andheri West'.

I read the message again and again and again, then tried to understand it again and again and again.

'Hey, Riya, are you done? I am ordering pizza. Which one do you want? Come out fast.'

I realized that I was inside the bathroom. I finished quickly and came out.

We had pizza for dinner, started watching some random movie on television, left it halfway, made love, though half-heartedly from my side that day.

◆

'This is not fair.' I picked up my phone and messaged.

I was in bed, feeling lazy, though not sleepy. Raghav left for work a little early in the morning. He had some preparations left before an important meeting, he said.

'What is not fair, madam, the message or the secret way I saw you without being seen? Just kidding.'

He knew my temper well. Whenever he felt I would get angry at him for having said whatever he wished to, he would say 'Just kidding'—an intelligent idea to cool down someone.

But that day I was really angry (though I was not sure). 'You didn't keep your promise.'

'The promise was not to meet you, by the way, and I didn't meet you.'

Suddenly I had a doubt. 'Are you sure you saw me, or was it someone else?' I chuckled.

'Blue jeans and red shirt. Yeah, I now feel it was someone else. Ha ha ha . . .'

That was what I wore yesterday. He was right, but I had many more things to ask. 'But, Neel, I never told you about my programme to Mumbai. How did you get to know about it? Or was it a mere coincidence?'

'Yeah, you didn't tell me the date and time, but you had mentioned that approximately after a month you will come to Mumbai. And you are a Jet Airways fan, I know that.'

'But still, how?'

'I have a friend in Jet Airways. I begged him to search in his Delhi–Mumbai passenger list for Riya Goyal, that's it. And after eight days of frustration, the list showed one such name. I thought it was worth trying.'

'Understood. One thing for sure today.'

'What?'

'That you are crazy!'

'So if you don't mind, will you please add this crazy friend's name in your phone book?'

'Yeah, and how did you manage to get my phone number?'

'Dr Riya Goyal, it's in your personal information page in Facebook, and I have it in my phone book for the last six months. I was not sure if someday my moody friend decides to block me on Facebook. I thought I should have some backup for emergency.'

'Ha ha ha . . . I guess Sunita has come. I am going.'

'Your maid? Okay, bye-bye.'

The days were moving, and the nights were flying. I still thought it was wrong. We should not talk to each other.

He used to message me sometimes, but I rarely, very rarely, replied.

I had enough in my life. I was in no mood to multiply the complications in it.

Chapter 16

Cheers and Fears

The programme was all set. Next weekend, Smiti was coming to stay with us. She called me on Thursday evening. 'Next week, done. Friday to Monday.'

'Are you sure, Smiti?' I almost screamed out of joy. 'You know what you just said.'

'Yes, I know. Friday to Monday,' she repeated. 'Gonna celebrate my birthday with my best friend.'

I was still perplexed. 'But what about Sameer?'

'Now, you have come to the point, I understood. Sameer had to prepone his flight by a week. He has to finish some more official formalities before he joins on 1 October there.'

'So when is he leaving now?'

'Day after tomorrow, Saturday.'

'Hurray!' I almost screamed. 'I am so excited.'

'Hey, girl, what do you mean? My fiancé is going to the other side of the globe, that too for three years, and you are excited? What for?' Both of us laughed and laughed.

'With all due respect to you, your fiancé, and your relationship, I am happy that after such a long, long time, we will be able to celebrate your birthday together. Only the two of us.'

'You are right. Those days were so cute. We had nothing—no degrees, no money—but we had time, a lot of time for each other.'

'Now, don't be emotional. We two will be together in one of our birthdays after, say, a decade? I am so excited,' I said.

'Not two, darling. Three. What about Raghav?'

'Hey, Raghav is flying to Paris straight from Delhi for two weeks. I forgot to tell you.'

'Ha ha ha. You know what? I feel I should ask when he is in Mumbai rather than asking when he is not. Ha ha ha. Just joking. Busy guy!'

'No, it's not a joke. I also want to ask the same question at times.'

And both friends laughed loudly from their hearts.

Friday came quickly without much delay. I had stuffed my fridge and kitchen with all that Smiti liked—chocolates, blueberry muffins, potato chips (American style), Magic Pops, Little Hearts, and *kaju katli*.

I packed her gift in a red-and-silver paper. There was a beautiful maroon off-the-shoulder party dress inside with an asymmetrical Swarovski neckpiece. I had already discussed with the Wills Lifestyle guy that if there were some size issues with the dress, he would exchange it, to which he didn't make any fuss.

With a final glance to the house to ensure perfection, I took my bag and keys and headed towards the airport.

Seeing Smiti after two long years was not less than a magical moment. Times might have changed, so as the places, but we had not changed, except that Smiti looked a bit more plumpish. *But she can still fit in the dress*, I thought.

As soon as she reached near me, we hugged each other out of joy. Without wasting much time, we drove home. There was so much to talk about, so much to share, and so much to celebrate.

We two kept on gossiping. We had a little wine with pizza, finished half of the snack stock, and finally went off to sleep at three in the morning.

After a few hours, Smiti's phone beeped for a message, one more, and one more. Half asleep, I searched her phone and gave it to her. It beeped again, but the sound was coming from far.

'Not mine. These are your messages, mad girl. Your phone is in front of the television.'

I got up, surprised. Yes, she was right. It was my phone. One more message. She screamed, 'Please, Riya, put it on silent mode. Let me sleep.'

'Can't. What if Raghav calls?'

She got up, sat on the bed, holding a pillow on her lap. Suddenly her sleepy eyes became interested in the topic. 'That means this is not Raghav . . . So who is this desperate soul sending you messages after messages so early in the morning?'

'By the way, my dear friend, it's not early. It's already nine, you see?' And I drifted towards the bathroom.

'Hey, come here. Don't change the topic.'

'A colleague. Wait, I will ask him what's so urgent.'

Smiti seemed suspicious, but she kept quiet.

'Yeah, hello, Aditya. What's so urgent? Okay, but I can't come for the party today. My friend is here, and I am gonna spend all the time with her.'

Neel was surprised but understood. 'Is it so? What about tomorrow? We can postpone the party for you, madam.' His tone sounded gleeful. He seemed to take advantage of the moment and my perplexity.

I pretended again. 'I told you I can't come. Tell him sorry from my side. I have plans with my best friend tomorrow.'

'Where?'

'Harbour Bar, the Taj, for her birthday. Only we two.' Without realizing it, I told everything. I can't say whether it was the effect of wine in the night or sleep deficit.

'No problem. Some other time.'

'Bye.' And I kept the phone. That was Neel on the other side of the phone.

Smiti got a doubt, I guess. She was always smarter than me. She snatched the mobile from my hand.

'You said "Aditya". But here it reads "Neel". You are hiding something from me.'

I had told Smiti in the night a bit about my friendship with Neel and also about the promises we made.

Now there was no way to hide it. I had to tell her the part two of the story.

'Despite the promise, he somehow managed to get a glimpse of me the day I landed up here. He took my phone number from my Facebook personal info page. He messages me almost every two to three days. However, mostly I don't reply. But yes, sometimes I do.'

'Do you like him?' This was too straight a question for me.

I waited for a moment, balanced myself, and said, 'Does it matter, Smiti? I am married. This question would have made sense if he had come into my life five years ago.'

'Right, you are, but since you came back, it never stopped. What does it mean?'

'You see, I am sure I am never going to meet him in person. Men are different. They lose interest fast. He will also forget me with time once he finds a girl for himself. And he will. He has all the qualities a girl can ask for.' I smiled. Sensing the artificiality in my smile, Smiti asked, 'And what about you?'

'Nothing. I am married, and Raghav is my husband. That's the eternal truth.' I paused. 'Neel is a friend, a good friend. I talk to him, message him only when Raghav is not there. Once I start working, I will also not have much time.'

'Oh I see, so Neel is a timepass, just a timepass.'

'Shut up, please. I don't want to hurt him. That's why I talk to him. Once he finds someone else, I will stop. I know my limits.'

'The only thing I can infer with surety from all this is that you are confused, as usual.'

'Don't we have something else to discuss?' I wanted it to end now.

Smiti had already fixed an appointment with some gynaecologist, Dr Anuradha Bhandari, at St Luke's Hospital and Research Centre after listening to my HPV story in the evening.

We arrived thirty minutes ahead of our appointment time and made a file on my name from the registration desk.

'Mrs Riya Goya.' My name was called on a loudspeaker. We two headed towards the doctor's chamber.

As the nurse opened the door for us, I saw a neat room with lots of thank-you cards and pictures of newborn babies all around the room pinned to the wall board, kept on the top of the cupboard, stuck on its door, and also on the table and under the glass on the table. An elegant, charming lady in her mid-thirties was sitting on the main chair on the other side of the table, facing us. Her light-blue sari was only a bit visible through her white apron. She looked impressive with neatly folded hair in a bun and a matching blue bindi on her forehead.

'Good morning. Have a seat, please.' Her cheerful voice distracted my attention from the decor, and we both sat down.

I repeated my whole HPV story to her.

She asked me many weird questions, like about vaginal discharge, excessive bleeding during periods, pain in the abdomen, if anyone was diabetic in my family, or if anyone had cancer. Though I couldn't understand why, I answered, and she documented all of it in my file.

Then she opened a PowerPoint-animated slide in her desktop, turned the screened towards us, and explained, 'You see, women who are sexually active, they have a very high chance of getting HPV infection, but in around 80 per cent of cases, which is a huge number, this infection gets cleared off automatically, in a time span of, say, one and a half to two years. But in those 20 per cent where it remains for longer time, the DNA of HPV gets incorporated into the DNA of our cells, and it starts causing some changes in the morphology and functioning of our cells now. These changes can be picked up by a Pap test, wherein we scrape some cells from your cervix, put it in a glass slide, and see it under a microscope.' She looked at me to ensure I understood.

And she continued, 'Now, going back to those 20 per cent who keep on harbouring the HPV for a long time, they develop changes at the cellular level, which is called as a low-grade lesion. Usually, this lesion, also in half of the cases, in due course of time is self-limiting. That means if you repeat a Pap smear after two years, it would come normal, but in the rest 50 per cent, it might remain as such or progress to become a high-grade lesion. These high-grade lesions are a bit dangerous as most of them will become cancer if not treated. But still, this is not a hard-and-fast rule.'

My mind had stopped working halfway because I was getting a Pap smear just to confirm that the HPV had not caused damage to the cells and tissue inside me. I was an optimistic girl, and my optimism had worked most of the time.

She closed the file and asked, 'Will you go and pass urine? Then go to room number 5. I will do an internal examination and do a Pap test.'

I pulled Smiti's hand and asked, 'What is this? What will she do with my urine now?'

'She won't do anything with your urine. Before internal examination, you have to empty your bladder so that the organs can be assessed properly.'

I followed the instruction and entered room number 5. There, a nurse was waiting for me. She asked me to remove my pants and my undergarments and lie down on the table. I had anticipated this. I lay down, and she covered my lower half with a green cotton sheet.

She went to call the doctor. Doctor Bhandari came. She examined my eyes, checked my pulse, and palpated my breast from outside my top as she did with my belly. Wearing gloves, she told me, 'Look, Riya, now I will do an internal examination for you. It's not a painful procedure at all, but you might feel a discomfort if you don't relax and cooperate. So relax, keep your buttocks down, and slide down to the edge of the table. She pulled a metal stool to sit so as my bottom was facing her. I felt embarrassed. She touched my thigh with her gloved hand and stood up. 'Riya, like this it is not possible. You have to relax. You see, if I forcibly examine you, firstly, you will have pain, and secondly, your report won't come correct. Do you understand?'

I had understood everything, but it was easy for her to say and difficult for me to do it. *How do I relax like this?* I thought.

She sat again, tried, and got up. Understanding something, she asked, 'Do you want Dr Smiti to come inside? Maybe you will feel more comfortable.'

I felt happy. 'Please call her.'

Smiti came inside. She smiled at the doctor, held my hand, looked in my eyes, and said, 'This is for you, baby. You know the importance.'

Now I could relax all my muscles. I closed my eyes and started taking deep breaths.

I felt no pain, just a funny feeling. Something cold was going inside me slowly, and I had a feeling as if my vaginal tissues were getting stretched apart. Then something was withdrawn out. The doctor stood up and smiled. 'That's it. Was it difficult?'

I smiled. 'No.' Next moment, I saw what she kept on the tray. Shit, a steel thing around ten centimetres long with two broad blades looking like a metallic beak of a huge bird, with nuts and bolts. 'If I had known that this was going to go inside me, I would have run out of this room.' All three laughed on my remark—Smiti, the doctor, and the nurse.

Chapter 17

Surprise Gifts and Surprises

It was twelve o'clock midnight of one of the most-awaited days. The day of surprises and celebrations started. As soon as I said 'Happy birthday', her phone rang.

'Thank you. Thank you. Love you. Miss you so much.' It was obvious Sameer was on the other side of the line. Talking to him, she went to the balcony. It gave me time to arrange the surprises. I brought her favourite blueberry cake from the fridge, arranged it on the table with candles and gifts.

She came back smiling, hugged me, and said thank you. After the cake, she opened the gifts. I could read the merriness on her face. We played music and danced for hours as we used to do when we were small.

We got up late, as was the routine these days, had a light breakfast, and headed for shopping, shopping, shopping, and more shopping. Nothing can give a girl more pleasure than shopping. Some say it's therapeutic, and I completely agree to it.

We had coffee, we had ice cream, and we also had *Lakhnavi* chat at one of the mall corners. By four in the afternoon, we were dead tired.

The evening plan was decided—7 p.m. at the Taj Mahal Palace, only the two of us.

Harbour Bar, the Taj Mahal Palace and Tower, Apollo Bunder, Colaba, Mumbai, at 7 p.m.

Smiti had decided to wear her new maroon dress with the neckpiece which I had gifted her. It fitted her well. I was dressed more simply with my black stilettos, blue denims, and blackish-blue top with full sleeves and a deep round neck. My small pendant and ear studs were made up of a conglomerate of multiple tiny diamonds, giving it a look of solitaire.

As we entered, a well-dressed girl guided us to a pre-booked table for two. The lights were minimum, interiors luxurious, and the ambiance calming. The instrumental music being played was extremely soothing to the ears, and the place smelled perfectly pleasing. The Gateway of India looked even more attractive from inside.

We refreshed the old memories, shared the beautiful moments, planned her wedding, and were enjoying delicious titbits. Margarita sips were adding on to the relaxed pleasure.

I had one more surprise for her, which I had just picked up on the way and had lied that it was a shirt which Raghav had told me to pick up. I handed over the packet to her. She opened it with surprise. There was this T-shirt with a picture of two tiny girls kissing each other exactly on their pouted lips. It was the two of us more than a quarter of the century ago, black and white. 'I am your best friend, and there isn't anything you can do about it' read the words at the bottom of the picture.

'Where did you get it from?'

'This year when *didi* went during Guriya's summer vacation to Almora, Mom showed all our childhood albums to her. She clicked the ones which she felt amazed with and sent a few to me too. Raghav made so much fun of me, looking at those. Do you remember how fat I was?'

'You were not fat. Who says? You were prettily plumpish.' She got up in urgency. Alcohol had started showing its diuretic effect. 'I am going to the washroom. Will be back in a minute.'

Smiti came back from the washroom and told me casually, 'Look, people have got so much money they come here alone also. This is not the place to come alone for a daily dinner.' She had sarcasm in her voice.

'Why? What do you mean?'

'Don't look there, but there is a boy sitting straight across our table. I am noticing him for a long time. He is all alone. He was here even before we came.'

She had instructed me strictly not to look, but it's human mind. If you tell it not to do something, it wants to do exactly the same, so I looked in the said direction from the angle of my eyes. 'I feel I have seen him somewhere,' I whispered, trying to remember.

'Ha ha . . . Maybe some small-time star or celebrity. Otherwise, who will come here to such a costly place alone to have a daily dinner? You must have seen him on television or in some magazine. Leave him alone now.'

Though I agreed to Smiti, my mind kept on wondering, *Who is he?*

With a strike of the next moment, I got up, went near that table, and stood there. Seeing me, the man got up, surprised.

'Hello. May I help you?'

Confused, Smiti was also there by now.

When he looked at me, I lost all my confidence and got confused. 'I think I know you.'

'Is it? How?' He seemed calm as if it kept on happening to him now and then.

'I am sorry. I think I got confused. Your face resembles to one of my childhood friends, so I got confused. I am sorry.'

Out of jealousy or disbelief, I don't know why Smiti hit me hard on my back with her fist.

'Ouch, what are you doing?'

'Nothing. By the way, who is this childhood friend whom I don't know?' she whispered in my ear.

The man couldn't control his laughter. 'You are cuter in real.'

'Neel! I knew this was you.'

'Neel?' Smiti nearly shouted with big question marks in her eyes.

'But I was not here with any bad intention. When you disclosed your programme over the phone that day, I couldn't resist. I think you were half asleep that day. Otherwise, you are so secretive. I didn't want to lose the chance to feel you around.' He gave a smile full of affection.

'Smart guy, but crazy, I will say,' Smiti said.

We all sat down.

He shook hands with Smiti. 'Happy birthday. Sorry, I didn't bring a gift. I was very confident that I won't be caught.'

I was feeling nice and thrilled but also cold and wobbly.

I don't know how many times he said 'I am sorry. Don't misunderstand me. I didn't mean to do this. My intentions were not this.'

After we had enough of it, Smiti said, 'We will take it as it was just a coincidence. Stop blaming yourself and feeling bad now.'

Smiti's phone rang. She received the call, blushed, got up, and went towards an open area.

We two, sitting across the table, had no words, I guess. Then I noticed something. 'Stop looking there.'

'What?' He felt conscious.

'You know what very well.'

'Hey, your solitaire is pretty.'

'That's not a solitaire. Tiny diamonds together to fool others.' I smiled confidently. If you ever want to divert the attention of a girl, just appreciate her dress or jewellery, and the topic will change itself.

'Whatever.'

'I know what you were looking at. Don't play smart with me.'

'Sorry, but you are beautiful. I must admire.'

'I am not talking to you any more. All men are the same.' I made an irritated face.

'So what? I didn't do or say anything. Why don't you pull your top a little up? Not my fault.'

I didn't speak. I pulled my top from behind so that the neckline came up.

'Okay. Do one thing—take these forks and make me blind. That's the only punishment for me.' He took two forks from the table, one on each hand, and showed me.

I started laughing. 'It's okay.'

By the time, Smiti joined. We had the dinner together. Neel insisted on paying the bill and didn't listen to any of the logics.

Around eleven thirty, we left. We went home straight from there. Smiti looked at me and said on the way back, 'It was my best birthday ever.'

For me, it felt like the best day ever.

Chapter 18

How Much Is Too Much?

Next day, Smiti left. Raghav was still in Paris, so practically, I had nothing to do for the next one week.

Let's use this time for something constructive, I thought. It had been more than two months since I had come back from Holland. I had really enjoyed every moment with Maa, Baba, Vartika, and Raghav also. I had met Mom, Dad, didi, jiju, and Guriya. Even with Smiti, I had the much-awaited lovely weekend. Doctor's appointment was also over.

Now, what's next? Time to focus on career. I had already decided that I would be joining the JLN Institute again. Reasons are many—it's close to my place, I am used to the environment, Professor Thakur carries a good opinion about me, and he had already offered me a post as faculty.

Since I came here, I had not met the professor, so I thought of calling him.

'Good morning. Good morning. How are you, Dr Goyal?'

'I am fine, sir. Came back a couple of weeks ago from Delhi. Wanted to meet you.'

'Oh sure. What have you thought about my job offer?'

'Yes, sir. I want to join. Moreover, my husband wants to continue his business from Mumbai for at least the next five years.'

'That's good news and good time in that case. We are advertising faculty posts next week. You better come with your documents and discuss with me.'

'Yeah, for sure. What will be a good time to meet you, sir?'

'Today afternoon? Around three?'

'Perfect. I shall be there.'

I searched the almirah, the drawer. *Where is the file with all my certificates and documents? I always keep it here in the third rack from above.* I was getting a bit restless.

Maybe Raghav has locked it in that big cupboard for the sake of its safety in my absence. I started searching for the key but couldn't find it anywhere. *Raghav is in Paris, how do I ask him?* I was getting more and more panicky. *I have been called at three today. What am I going to show him and discuss?*

'Sunita . . .' I called the maid as I got an idea.

She came running to the bedroom on hearing my voice. 'Jee didi.'

'Can you go across the road? There is a small locksmith's shop at the corner. Have you seen it? Please go and call him. I have to open this cupboard urgently, and the keys are missing.'

'Yes, didi. I will call him.'

Within fifteen minutes, Sunita was there with a boy, the key-maker.

He tried many keys, many wires, and ultimately after a struggle, he could open the lock.

'Thank you, bhaiya. How much?'

'No problem, madam. I will make a proper key for it and give it to you tomorrow. You can pay for that.'

'Okay, fine.' I agreed, and he left. Sunita had already gone to finish her pending work in the kitchen.

I started searching my file in the open cupboard. It was not seen there too. Out of irritation, I started throwing clothes outside one by one. Having thrown a few, I realized this was not my stuff, but all this was a girl's stuff. 'Shit, what is this?'

I screamed again, 'Sunita . . .'

She came running. 'What happened, didi?'

'What is all this? Whose clothes are these? These are not mine.'

'I don't know, didi.'

'Call the laundry fellow. He must have made the mistake, and Raghav hadn't realized it in my absence.'

By the time I finished my statement, Sunita was holding a cloth or two, sitting on her knees on the floor, trying to identify them. She said, 'Don't call the laundry, didi.' She paused, looked at my face, and continued, 'These are that other madam's clothes, I think.'

'Which other madam?' I was horribly confused.

'Didi, I wanted to tell you this, but I was scared that you will scold me. When you were not here, one madam stayed here with Raghav bhaiya. Wherever bhaiya used to go, she accompanied him.'

'Are you sure? Have you seen her with your own eyes?'

'Yes, didi. She was not Indian, I think. She couldn't speak very good Hindi, so she hardly spoke to me. She spoke in English to Raghav bhaiya all the time. And I could not understand anything they were talking about.'

'Do you know her name?'

'No, didi.'

But I knew it was none other than Sara.

I cried the whole day. I postponed my appointment with Professor Thakur, stating that I was not feeling well.

I had no pain and was not in trauma, but still I felt sick . . . very sick inside.

I realized it was time. Time to talk to Raghav. Enough is enough.

Tuesday morning at around four, Raghav arrived home from Paris. He slept to get up only at around ten. He was getting ready to go to the office, but if he went to the office, that meant he would come back only in the night and would be tired. Dinner and then bed. I wanted to talk to him before bedtime, for sure.

During breakfast, I said, 'Raghav, don't go for work today.'

He preferred to finish his *aloo paratha* and the headlines in the newspaper, after which he looked at me and asked, 'Why?' He was surprised, as I had never made this demand so obvious before.

'Cos I want to talk to you.'

'Can we talk in the evening?'

'No. It's urgent.' My voice was stern.

'Okay. In that case, tell me now.'

'Do you love me?' I looked at him straight in his eyes.

'Why this question suddenly today?'

'Please answer. This is important for me to know.'

'Yes,' he said.

'Then what about Sara?'

This one he had not expected, it looked like. He folded his newspaper and kept it aside. 'What do you want to say? You have spied enough during your planned stay at Kanpur. I guess you know everything.'

'But I did not believe it. I want to hear the truth from you.'

'Okay, as you wish.' He continued, 'I know Sara for the last ten years. I met her in Moscow during an official meeting. We fell in love. The plan was simple—to get married. But my parents, you know them, they are stubborn. They didn't agree. Sara came to India only for me. She had nowhere else to go. She joined my office in New Delhi and worked for me.' He paused. 'I was very confident that things will settle down slowly. I tried to convince Maa, Baba, but they were dead against the marriage. Though they didn't mind Sara coming home or me meeting her, I think they were scared that they will lose their only son if they complained. Foolish I kept on taking that as a positive and progressive sign from their side.'

'But when you were so sure about her, why did you marry me? That's the question.'

'Will you wait? I am telling you everything. We waited for five long years for my parents to get adjusted to it, but they couldn't understand. They started forcing me to get married. Then one day I put my foot down, saying that if not Sara, I am not going to marry anyone else. Then the Indian drama followed. Baba said he will commit suicide if I married Sara, a Russian girl, that too a divorcee. Maa said she will eat poison if I say I will not marry anyone else now. She can't stand it if people would say that her son is a gay.'

He paused again. 'I went in some sort of depression and was on treatment for almost a year. I had no other choice. Parental pressure was too much, so I had to marry you.'

There were tears in my eyes. 'But my life got ruined in all that.'

'If you were so troubled with all this, why didn't you complain? You have known about Sara way back when you were in Kanpur. I got a hint not from you but from Maa and Vartika.'

'Yeah, I knew that Sara existed. But, Raghav, I didn't know that she is sharing my room, my bed, and my husband even now.' Then I told the whole event—how, during the search for my missing files, I discovered all her stuff locked in my cupboard.

'Don't pretend, Riya. You had the idea that I was in Paris with her.'

'What?' I was stunned. 'No.'

'Yes. I had kept the tickets on the living room table for more than a week for you to see. I didn't want to cheat on you.'

'Horrible it is.' My voice was sounding more and more irritated. 'I don't spy on you. Why should I check your tickets? And what did you just say? Will you please repeat it? You are not cheating on me? So what does all this mean, Mr Raghav Goyal?'

'Sit down and listen to me carefully. If you couldn't guess the meaning of my coming home late, disappearing off and on, and my frequent trips with you knowing Sara at the backdrop, it's your fault, not mine.'

'Oh, I know. Now, what's next, Mr Goyal?'

'Depends on you. I have given you everything—all the respect, love, and position that a wife deserves. For the society and for the world, I am your husband, and it's not that I don't love you.'

'Love? This is not love. Even if you start living with a dog, you tend to develop a bond with it, but that's not called love.'

'But I can't leave Sara either. She has left her country, her people, everything for me. Without any expectations ever.'

'Oh, I see.'

'Moreover, going back to your parents is not an option for an Indian married woman, I guess. Why do you want to hurt everybody and defame your family as well as mine? God wanted it this way. And everything is fine, only if you try to understand and adjust a bit.'

I had nothing to say. I needed time. Time to think.

Surprisingly, Raghav came early from office that day, but by that time, I had already shifted my stuff in the guest room.

I wanted an angel to come and splash water on this messed-up canvas to flush off the colours; I wished to paint the story again.

Chapter 19

The Much-Awaited Report

Next week, my Pap smear report was expected. I called the hospital. A lady at the reception asked, 'Mrs Riya Goyal, hospital number 253609?' I checked it and said, 'Yes, correct.'

'Your report is ready. You may come and collect it. Should I fix your appointment with the doctor?'

'Yes, please.'

'Oh, you have been consulting Dr Bhandari, but she is on vacation till the 30th. So do you want to wait till then?'

'Is it? Do I have any other option? I don't want so much delay.'

'Yes, you may show it to Dr Sheetal Mehra. She is available and is taking care of Dr Bhandari's cases in her absence.'

'Okay, in that case, can you please fix an appointment for tomorrow morning?'

'Yes, I will do that. So tomorrow, 14 September, your appointment is at 9 a.m.'

I reached the OPD at eight thirty. There were still thirty minutes to wait. I had come alone so had nothing to do. I just sat quietly in the waiting area and started noticing the surroundings.

It was a nicely lit rectangular waiting area with four rooms on each side along the longer arms. Chairs were arranged parallel to the smaller arms of the rectangle for the patients. On the centre, there was a tall table with a round base. On top of the table, a flower pot with white and yellow gerberas with lush green leaves was stationed. Below it were three circular shelves in horizontal planes. The first shelf had newspapers, the second one had health magazines, and the last one had patient information pamphlets. The walls were painted in two shades of yellow, which made the area look brighter. There were framed posters on the walls depicting issues related to obstetrics and gynaecology. The left wall demonstrated the dos and don'ts during pregnancy and breastfeeding, while the right wall showed the importance of cervical cancer screening, vaccination, and something about urinary incontinence and bleeding problems.

Today the air was not like the other day when I had come along with Smiti. I could sense a palpable chaos around. Two nurses were running from room to room. The rush was much more. Two girls wearing aprons, who looked like junior doctors, were sweating stress and irritation. When I concentrated a bit, I could hear a patient's scream from room number 4 in front of me, intermixed with some shouting in a husky feminine voice.

In a moment, the same door opened, and the things became comprehensible. I saw the senior consultant for today, Dr Sheetal Mehra, walking out of the room, followed by a scared patient on the verge of crying.

Dr Mehra was a tall, slim lady wearing a beautiful *Kanjivaram* sari with big *nakshatra*-like diamonds in her ears. She looked like in her early fifties. Her walk was bold, and her body language, hostile. She had only one expression on her face—anger mixed with irritation, mixed with pride. It appeared as if her smile and kindness got digested and assimilated years ago by the hunger of fame and possession.

Then my turn came. On call, I went inside with the file. She was in a hurry. She opened my file and read my Pap smear report, 'LSIL (possibility of HSIL cannot be ruled out).' Handing over the file to the nurse, she said, 'Sister, colposcopy at three today,' and she left the room. I couldn't understand a bit of it. *What is my report? What did she say to the sister, and now, what is at three today?*

The nurse seemed to sense my state of mind and said, 'Come with me.' She took me to one of the examination rooms and tried to explain, 'Your report has some abnormal result, so one more test has to be done with a camera.'

What the hell? Now what is this? I thought. 'I want to talk to the doctor properly. She left the room without talking to me. How could she?' I asked in irritation.

The nurse calmed me down. 'She is a very senior doctor. She won't explain. Rather, she will start shouting at you and me too.'

'But I need to talk to someone.'

'Do you want to talk to the junior doctors?'

I agreed, but the nurse didn't return for what seemed like an hour. Neither did any junior doctor come. I saw them rushing here and there, talking to other patients and doing their routine work in between in a hustle.

And then the same nurse came to me after around one hour or more and said, 'All doctors are very busy. Madam is not in a good mood. She is upset with everybody and everything, so it is taking time.'

By then, I had already decided, having discussed my report and my concerns with Smiti. I preferred to leave and take another appointment after the 30th, once Dr Bhandari was back.

It was 1 October. It was the same place, but it looked so different today, cool and calm. Patients were seated comfortably, waiting for their turn. Nurses looked more fresh and relaxed.

Then I saw the much-awaited Dr Bhandari walking through the corridor. Some patients greeted her, and some just smiled. She wore a continuous smile on her face in an effort to respond to each and every one there. She was simply but elegantly dressed as before.

She looked at me. 'You are Dr Smiti's friend, if I am not wrong. Please come inside. Smiti had called and told me that you wanted to discuss your report.'

She saw my report. 'Hmm . . . so it says that most likely the HPV has started affecting your cells.'

'What's next, Doctor?'

'Mostly, it is a low-grade lesion. However, the pathologist has seen some changes which are seen in high-grade lesion.'

'Is it something really serious, Doctor?'

'You see, the report of the Pap smear just tells us whether you are at low risk or high risk of developing the disease. It is only a screening process. But once the screening report shows anything other than normal, we need to confirm it with a biopsy or by taking a chunk of the tissue and examining it.'

'But what I know is, in the screening test, if it comes low risk, we don't need to do anything, isn't it?'

'You are absolutely right, Riya.'

'So is it because my report says that there is a possibility for it to develop into a higher lesion?'

'Actually, not because of that. I will try to explain it to you. You see, unlike other screening tests, Pap test doesn't have a very good sensitivity, so if your report comes low grade also, it still has a chance of having high-grade lesions in around 10–15 per cent of cases. If the report comes abnormal, either high or low grade, we would want to see your whole cervix under magnification using a machine called colposcope. If it looks normal or correlates with low-grade lesion, we will just keep you on follow-up, but if by chance it looks abnormal, we will have to take a biopsy.'

'And what if the biopsy report comes abnormal?'

'Abnormal report may be either low grade (also called CIN 1) or high grade (CIN 2, 3). If it is low grade, you just need a follow-up.'

'You mean to say that if it is high grade, it needs some more treatment?'

'Yes, as I had shown you last time, this category is very close to frank malignancy in the natural history of cervical cancer. We have to manage it more aggressively.'

My head started aching.

'So what do you suggest me to do now?'

She thought something for a while and opened the file again and said, 'Riya, if I have to summarize your case, you are twenty-nine years, married for four and a half years, no children, no significant past or family history, totally asymptomatic. However, incidentally you were found to have an infection with a high-risk HPV, type 16. Pap smear shows a low-risk/high-risk picture.' She paused and smiled cunningly though sweetly. 'You created quite a good fuss during your pelvic examination last time.'

I felt a bit embarrassed. 'Doctor, please try to understand. I didn't do it intentionally.'

'Yeah, I do understand, Riya. What I am telling you is, you get admitted. Under slight sedation, I will do your colposcopy and, if required, biopsy in the operation theatre because I doubt you will allow me to take a biopsy in the OPD.'

'Sounds better.' I agreed.

'So get admitted on Monday evening. I will post you on Tuesday as the first case in OT, and then you can go home the same evening.

'Perfect,' I said.

'But someone has to be there with you to sign the consent forms. Your husband, maybe.'

'Sure,' I said.

I was home, waiting for Raghav. I had not told him anything about the HPV or the Pap test because I didn't feel like telling him. But now I had to. Now I needed his company and at least his consent. I had no one else who could possibly accompany me this time.

So I told him in short, 'Raghav, I have a request. A few days ago, Smiti and I went for routine gynaec check-up, and incidentally, they found some problem with my Pap test, so I have to get a colposcopy and biopsy done this Tuesday. That means Monday evening, admission, and discharge on Tuesday after the procedure.'

After I had shifted to another room, we were not talking to each other more than what was essentially required.

He looked at me and gave a sarcastic smile. 'You are a modern girl. You have survived in Europe for six months all alone. Then why do you need my company for one day in the hospital?'

I was truly irritated with his rudeness. 'I don't need company to enjoy my life. The doctor needs you to come to sign the consent form.'

'Yes, I will come to sign those. I am your husband. I will fulfil all my duties, but don't expect me to stay there overnight. I have enough work to finish for the coming delegation.'

I kept quiet.

'Maybe you could have fixed this for next week. You could have called your mom to stay with you for some days. I would have booked her tickets.'

I didn't feel like saying anything at that moment.

So he came with me on Monday to the hospital, completed the formalities, and left. While going, he said, 'Call me when I should come and pick you tomorrow. I have given the number in the reception. They will call me if there is anything.'

'Thank you,' I said.

'Take care.' And he left me all alone in the empty room with scary thoughts.

Surprisingly, I missed Neel today more than I missed anyone else. I called him, and we spoke as if everything was normal. I was afraid that if I told him the truth, he would come to the hospital.

I tried to be as normal as I could sound, though he was expert in sensing my anxiousness and my distress. I told him not about the hospital but gave him a hint about the conflict with Raghav without revealing any details.

At the end of the conversation, I found myself happily laughing. I thought, *It doesn't matter who hurt you or who broke you down; what matters is that there is someone who will make you smile again.*

I don't remember when I fell asleep. I was not supposed to eat anything in the morning. At half past eight, they wheeled me inside the operation theatre. This was my first experience of any such thing. I saw four men with green masks and caps bending over my face as I lay down still on the OT table, wearing a blue gown and blue cap provided by the hospital. A man among those explained something to me, though I didn't understand a word. And in seconds, a transparent plastic mask covered my mouth and nose. I was asked to count 10, 9, 8, 7, 6, 5 . . .

Then I remember someone saying, 'Wake up, Riya, it's over,' patting on my cheeks. I opened my eyes as if from the deepest sleep ever.

Sometime later, Dr Bhandari came to the post-operative recovery room in her OT attire with a cap and mask, though the mask was loosely hanging on her neck now. She asked, 'Riya, is everything okay?'

I nodded. 'What did you see, Doctor?'

'It looked fine to me. Nothing to worry about. But I have taken small biopsies from two suspicious-looking areas.'

'When will I come to know the report?'

'This report will come to me directly. I will mail you as soon as I get it.'

I called Raghav, and he drove me home.

Sometimes when things appear to be falling apart, they might be falling in place.

Chapter 20

Stronger Bonds

My life was hanging in the centre of a triangle—the three points being Raghav with Sara, Neel with my illusions, and my self-concern with HPV. My relationship with Raghav was defined, but suffocating. Whatever I had with Neel was hazy, though soothing. HPV and the ongoing story was the truth, but painful.

When I started thinking, one point became gigantic, and the other two shrunk. Then suddenly the other point started growing big, and the other two shrunk. I felt as if I was being pushed, pulled, and finally being torn apart.

I called Neel out of desperation so that I could be free of my thoughts, my fears, and my imaginations. 'Hi.'

'Hi, Riya. What happened? Hope you are fine.'

'Just felt like calling you.'

'Yeah, you can call me anytime. My heart feels happy to hear your voice.'

'But I am not feeling that happy, Neel. Can I share something with you? Only if you have some time.'

'I have all the time in the world today. I had applied a compensatory off today for working on Sunday. You are not sounding good. Do you want to meet? What's the matter, Riya?'

125

'If you have time, I want to share a few secrets which I do not dare to share with anyone. Can't tell it to Mom, Dad, and didi. They will get depressed. I thought of Smiti, but I didn't feel like telling her everything.'

'You can count on me, Riya.'

'At least I know you won't judge me for whatever I tell you.'

'I promise.'

I told him the whole story—how my inquisitiveness revealed I was having HPV infection, how that led to finding clues about someone in Raghav's life, how I discovered the Russian divorcee Sara's story, how I got my Pap test done which had now come positive, about Raghav's opinion about his relationship with Sara and me, and my perplexed, screwed-up future.

'I am surprised, Riya. You always said I am your friend. You were going through so much and never told me.'

'I kept quiet.'

'I have an idea, Riya.'

'What?'

'Let's elope.'

I was about to keep the receiver down. He said, 'Okay, I am sorry. That was just a joke. I wanted you to smile. That's it.'

'Stupid joke,' I replied.

I was feeling much better after talking to him though. I should have done it before, much before, I thought.

'My life has been smooth throughout, Riya, more or less. You know everything about it. But there is one thing which changed my opinion about the powers and existence of God. It is about my mom, my most precious asset.'

'What?'

'Riya, my mother was diagnosed five years ago with breast cancer. I have seen a hell of a time. She was extremely upset after she was diagnosed with it to an extent that she developed suicidal tendencies.'

'Oh, I am so sorry.'

'She is a very health and beauty-conscious lady. My father used to tease her that she had become fat when I was there in her tummy, and she got so horrified with that look of hers that she dropped her plans of becoming pregnant ever again.'

'How is she now?'

'She is still on treatment. It was not in the late stage, but the doctor advised surgical removal of her breast, which made her extremely upset.'

'Hmm, I understand.'

'I have seen my father and mother going through a horrible phase in life, so I decided to never leave them. They are my priority in life now.'

'How was she diagnosed to have that?'

'That's why I thought to tell you. She used to feel a tiny lump in her breast, but she ignored it for weeks and months. She had read about it in the newspaper and seen on television, but she thought she can't have cancer. And ultimately, when she decided to show it to the doctor, it required complete removal of her breast.'

'Sad.'

'I just want you to understand, Riya, life is very unpredictable and, at times, can be very painful. Hurdles are a part of our lives. How we come out of the problems is what is important, not the problem.'

'You are right, Neel.'

'You may be going through a bad phase in your life now— be it Sara or your test report—but have faith. One day, every problem will be sorted out. Let your faith be bigger than your problems.'

'Test report will be sorted out soon, I know, but not Sara.'

'Okay, madam, tell me, what do you want me to do? Should I kidnap her or do something else to finish the story?' He laughed cunningly. 'Anything for you, madam.'

I laughed with him. 'No need. You will kidnap her, and then you will have to keep her all your life. She has no plans to go back to Russia, Raghav told me.'

'No problem. In that case, I will keep her with me.'

'Shut up. You deserve a better girl, not her.'

'Oh yeah. Do you know? I think I have found one.'

'What do you mean? Who is she?'

'Actually, Riya, she is an old friend. But day by day, I feel I am falling for her. I haven't told her yet because I have to talk to my parents before I can commit anything.'

'That's good news. Why didn't you tell me before?' I was trying to show my happiness, but I was feeling as if I was being strangulated inside. I don't know why.

'Good question. Tell me one thing—after coming back to India, in more than three months, for how many minutes have we spoken to each other?'

'I agree. Okay, congratulations, a heartiest one.'

'That's not enough, for this, I want to take you for a treat. Would you like to meet her?'

My words got stuck. I couldn't say yes; I couldn't say no. Rather, I asked, 'What's her name?'

'Riya, I am getting a call from Mom. I will call you later.'

'Okay.' I hung up.

It was not his fault. I only misunderstood him. He spoke to me with love, and I thought it was love.

I sat on the rocking chair near the window and thought, *Human mind is so complex. It wants things to happen, but still, it gets upset when it happens. Why am I upset if Neel has found a girl? It was bound to happen one day. I should be happy for him.*

Now maybe my life will be a little less complicated. My health issue will get sorted out by the end of the month. Neel will marry, and after that, our relationship will be over forever. As far as Raghav is concerned, I need to think and plan it. I can't let it go just like that because that is the only thing in the triangle which is defined. Five years ago, I had tied the knot of commitment, love, divinity, and oneness with Raghav. I can't leave him just like that. I have to handle this tactfully. One day he has to realize that I am more important to him than a Russian divorcee girl. I am his wife, and she is a relationship with no name.

But why don't I like the thought of Neel being in love with someone else? Do I have a special place for him in my heart? It's not possible. At this moment of time, I so desperately wanted to meet him and hug him. What has happened to me? I now wanted to spend as much time as possible with him, at least till the time his girl permanently came to his life with a named relationship.

I wrote a message, 'Why didn't you tell me about your girl before? Now you owe me a coffee as your punishment.' After staring at my own message for two seconds, I pressed Send. I was having a weird feeling inside me when I thought of meeting Neel with his fiancé.

You may call it jealousy. I call it fear of losing you.

Chapter 21

Flip-of-the-Coin Day

He said, 'I owe you a coffee, and I want to show you my new apartment. So with your kind permission, I would like to take you home, madam! I promise I will drop you back in thirty minutes.'

His words worked like a magic balm on my throbbing head, and I agreed without any ifs and buts. I took a quick shower and slipped in my black denim and pink top. Twenty minutes later, he was there to pick me up. It was around thirty minutes of drive to his place, with office-time traffic. The lift was out of order, so we had to climb, I guess, twenty-to-twenty-five-odd steps to reach the third floor.

It was a small room but neatly arranged. I sat on the sofa. Straight away, he went inside the kitchen. I saw something like a pile of spiral-bound papers on the table. Just for curiosity's sake, I picked it up, and turning the pages, I found a tiny naked newborn growing into a teenager Neel. I forgot everything else and started laughing loudly. 'Is it you?'

He came running to extricate which secret I had found and bumped on the sofa. This was a collection of his pics which his mom had gifted him on his fifteenth birthday

with small poems in each page with rhyming words. I
started reading it loudly:

Papa's sunshine, Mama's moonlight . . .
You make our days beautiful and bright!

Suddenly my brain analysed something. I turned to him
and exclaimed, 'Oh, now I know from where these poetic
genes have come.' He smiled and looked straight into my
eyes and said, 'You know what? You are the second most
beautiful lady in this world.'

'So who is the first?'

Playfully he replied, 'Riya with her wild smile is the first
one.' We kept on looking at each other, and the moment
froze. The tips of his fingers touched my skin. He held my
face in his hands and kissed my forehead. A sharp wave of
electric current rushed inside my body. Lips were about to
experience the intimacy. It was the most bizarre feeling of my
life. Still holding my face, the next moment, he whispered, 'I
will drop you home. Coffee some other time. I can't afford
to lose you for such a silly reason.'

On the way back, none of us spoke a word. I was melting
inside. I felt he tried to look at me a few times, but I couldn't
respond back.

'Madam! Your stop is here. What's the plan?' He
chuckled. I felt embarrassed not to have realized that we had
reached my place. I got down, looked at him, and smiled.
Instead of bye, I said thanks and walked towards the gate.
He kept on standing there. As I latched the main gate, I
waved him goodbye. He smiled and drove away.

The next moment, I remembered why my head was
throbbing. I got the report today as an email sent from Dr

Anuradha Bhandari, the gynaecologist. It was a blank mail with an attachment. I opened it. It read: 'Histopathology: suggestive of CIN 2 (cervical intraepithelial neoplasia 2)'. I couldn't understand what this jargon of words meant. I remembered Dr Bhandari explaining to me all this with facts and figures before the test. It was something about low-grade lesion and high-grade lesion. I was sure my report was going to be normal, so I didn't really care about what she was talking. I was still in denial. *I can't have this. I can't have cancer or anything related to it. I am absolutely normal.* I banged my totally confused head thrice on the wall. Next moment, a thought came to my mind. *Maybe the report got exchanged or the sample got mixed up with someone else's.*

I called Dr Bhandari on her mobile. No one picked up. On the next ring, a male voice answered, 'Madam is operating. Is it something urgent?' I could hear Dr Bhandari's voice in the background. She asked, 'Who is that, Ravi?'

'Madam, some Riya Goyal,' he murmured.

'Okay, one minute. Tell her I will talk to her tomorrow. Nothing to worry. Don't panic!'

'Ah.' I took a deep breath. *It was a mistake, wrong report.*

Ravi repeated, 'Call madam tomorrow. Madam said not to worry.'

I was thirsty, so I took a bottle of water and poured half of it inside my drying throat. I felt lazy and tired. I opened my bun and curled in my bed. I got up in the evening when my phone rang. It was Neel with his invitation for Neel-made coffee, and what followed felt like living a lifetime in just two hours. 'You know you are in love when you can't sleep because reality is finally better than your dreams.'

My head was not aching any more. I felt it silky all over. Anyway, at least I knew my report was also normal.

Chapter 22

The Shocker

We were in Dr Bhandari's chamber, only the two of us. 'Look, Riya, I will say you are unfortunate on one hand for you got into this trap, which, in my practice here in India, I don't see in your age. But if you look at the other angle, whatever happened, it happened for good.'

'What good, Doctor?' I was feeling bleak.

'What I mean to say is, in India we don't have any organized screening for cervical cancer. Women are screened when they come to us for some other problem related to gynaecology. That usually happens around or after, say, forty years of age, so many women, when they come at that age, already have full-blown cancer.'

'How does it relate to me now?'

'I will again take you through the event, how it happens with age. During twenty to thirty years of age, women get HPV infection. Around the age of thirty to forty, they develop changes in their cells and tissues. And then finally, when they are beyond forty, they develop cancer, which progresses very quickly. Now in your case, if you hadn't done your HPV test, I don't think you would have come for your Pap test, as you had no symptom. So ten years down the line, you would have developed the cancer.'

133

'I understand.'

'So you are lucky, Riya. We have diagnosed your disease before it became cancer, and this pre-cancer stage of the disease is 100 per cent curable.'

'Is it?'

'Yes. So, Riya, rather than sulking, you should have an optimistic and positive attitude. You are among those lucky ones in whom the disease is caught in the stage where it is completely curable.'

I felt a bit better. 'But what is the treatment?'

'Now we have to remove a cone from your cervix. This means the entire area where cancer can arise from will be removed.'

'Another operation?'

'Yeah, a small one.'

'But after that, I will never have to think about it. Please tell me that. I am sick of all this, one event after the other.'

'That I can't say right now. We will remove a cone-shaped tissue from the inside of your cervix. This is the area where possibly the cancer arises. However, after removing the cone, we send it again to the pathologist, who tells us whether the margins are free or not and whether, in that full tissue, the disease has spread more than what we expected.'

'Doctor, tell me in simple words. If some abnormality comes in that report too, then what's next?'

'Maybe we will have to repeat the procedure or remove the entire uterus.'

'Doctor, please do me a favour—take out my uterus. I don't need all this. I have gone through enough.'

'But you are young, Riya. Try to understand. You don't have any child. Why do you want to remove your uterus when we can manage with less radical approaches?'

'You won't understand a patient's point of view. It is difficult to come to the hospital again and again for the same silly thing. Appointments, admissions, consent, discharge, and then waiting for the report. You can't understand the trauma I go through each day while waiting for the report, finally to know that that I need one more test.'

'Cool down, Riya. I will suggest you to go home, think, and discuss it with your family. Don't take any decision hurriedly.' She was still polite and poised.

I agreed, though I had already made up my mind.

I called Mom in the evening. 'Hello, *beta*. How are you? Is everything all right? You don't sound good today.'

Moms are amazing. They know everything even if you don't want to tell them. I needed Mama desperately today. I missed her like anything. I knew she would not be able to entangle the web of problems I had developed, but I wanted her to hug me and say everything will be fine.

'Nothing, Mama. Was just missing you.'

'Are you all right? Is Raghav fine? Hope my little girl didn't have a fight with him.'

'I am no more a little girl, Mama.' I tried to change the topic. 'How is didi now? How is the little master? And, Mama, what is Guriya's reaction for the baby now?'

Mama said, 'Didi is recovering well. Guriya is happy at times and jealous also at times. But this is natural when a sibling is born. Didi used to feel much more jealous when you were born. She was scolding Guriya yesterday, so I told her she is better than you at least.' We laughed.

'True, Mama. I remember we used to fight a lot as children. She thought you loved me more and vice versa.'

'One important thing, Riya. I was planning to go home this month end, as everything looks settled here. Didi is also okay. She feels she will be able to manage as the baby will become a month old by then.'

'So back to Almora? Yeah, Dad must be missing you.'

'That was the plan, actually, but your dad gave me an idea. From Delhi, I can come to Mumbai, stay for some time with you and Raghav. It has been a long time. Once I go back home, it will become difficult to plan it, as I am already halfway now. Your dad suggested me this.'

I thought for a while. I really wanted to be with her, but I was scared that she would then come to know everything. I wanted to sort it out in my own style. So I said, 'I think, Mama, I will only come to Almora. It has been more than three years, I guess, that I have come home. Moreover, I will meet Papa also. Anyway, I have not joined work, so this is the best opportunity.'

'Then bring Raghav also. Good idea.'

'I will ask him, though he seems to be very busy these days.'

'Try. It will be good.'

'Okay, Ma, I will finalize it and let you know.'

'Take care. Bye, beta.'

True they say that God can't be everywhere, and therefore, he made mothers. Their voices shower magic, and the wounds get healed naturally.

Chapter 23

It's My Final Decision

We were on our way back from Sahil's birthday party. Sahil is Raghav's friend, a dear one. Raghav asked, 'You didn't eat properly there. I was watching you. Is everything all right?'

Though nothing was all right, I nodded. 'Yes.'

'Ice cream?'

I smiled. Despite whatever differences we had, Raghav still cared for me, loved me. I couldn't blame him for Sara. Sometimes I feel he is better than me. He didn't hide anything, unlike me. And it was not that he willingly chose to marry me when Sara was already there in his life. He had no option left. He is a good son. He didn't hurt his parents, and for his parents' sake, he didn't dump a girl either. From his point of view, what he had done and what he was doing was right.

Forget all the reasons why it won't work. And believe the one reason why it will.

We went to Baskin-Robbins. It was like those days after marriage when I was not aware of all the smudgy things going in the background, though it existed that time too—Sara

137

and HPV both. The difference was only of awareness. I had accepted it today. Ignorance is bliss, real bliss!

He kept his hand above mine, which I had casually kept on the table, and asked, 'What, Riya? You look upset. Is it because of Sara?'

I looked at him. *How can a person act so innocent?* I thought. *What if I tell him about Neel? Will he react the same way as he wants me to for Sara?* But I was not in the mood to discuss all this now. This would only make things more complicated. I wanted to discuss this issue more tactfully.

So I told him, 'There are some issues which are more important to me now rather than other things.'

'Go on.'

'Raghav, I met Dr Bhandari. She told me that even the biopsies she took have come abnormal.'

He interrupted, 'I am surprised how you got into all this problem. You are young. You don't have any such family history related to cancer or things like that, I guess.'

I lost control on hearing this. 'What do you mean, Raghav? You had given me this bloody virus. And from where you got it, do you want to know? From your divorcee bitch who had got fucked by how many in Russia, only she knows.' I just got up with agitation.

'Do you know what you said just now?' He took the keys from the table and started walking towards the car.

I had no other option but to follow him. It was the first time that I could see hatred and anger in his eyes. Usually he is a cool guy with a bit of escapist attitude. Today I saw a different Raghav.

Once we were out of the hustle and bustle of the city, on the highway I said, 'Sorry, I didn't want to say this, but this is how it is scientifically. Sorry for my words. I am very upset.'

He didn't answer. To break the silence after sometime, I said, 'The doctor wants me to come for treatment next week, but I want to go to Almora. I will also bring Mom with me. I get scared to be in the hospital alone.'

'What treatment? Again hospitalization?'

'It's some high-grade lesion I have developed. If I don't take treatment, it has a high chance of progressing into a cancer within years.'

'Oh, so what is the treatment?'

'I have two options. Either a cone biopsy, but again, it has to be rigorously followed up. That means again appointments, internal examinations, waiting for reports. I can't go through all these again and again.'

'And what is the other option?'

'Hysterectomy. Removal of the uterus.'

He looked at me. Stunned. He stopped the car. Though lost in our conversation, I didn't realize that we were in front of our home. 'Do you know what you are saying?'

'Yes. I know.' My looks were stern.

'We have not yet started our family.'

Sarcasm just burst out. 'For that you have Sara.'

He opened the lock and entered the house. I went to the guest room—my room.

I had no remorse for what I said or what I had decided.

I changed, lay down on the bed, and started reading a random novel in the light of the overhead lamp. Otherwise, the room was dark, and the door was open.

I didn't realize when Raghav entered the room. He snatched the book from my hands and flung it. I was shocked. I had never seen him like this before. His eyes were red.

He shouted, 'Say it again.'

I didn't speak a word—out of shock, anger, or arrogance, I don't remember.

'What were you saying you will get your uterus removed? What for when you have an option of a more conservative approach?'

'Yeah, I know I have an option, but that option requires me to see a doctor every six months, which might end up with admission and some surgical procedures at times.'

'So?'

'So who will be there with me on those times? Because my husband is so busy. He has time only to sign the consent form, and he thinks he has done his job well.'

'Who dropped you to the hospital? And by the way, who brought you back? You forgot.'

'No, I didn't. And I didn't forget that night also when I was left in the hospital room to fight with my fears alone, all alone.'

'So what do you expect me to do? Sit the whole night holding your hand, leaving all my work? I am not that kind, you should have known that by now.'

'Yeah, I know your kind.' I was getting cynical.

'If it is so, let me make this clear from my side too. If you have decided that you will do what you want and you will make decisions on your own, what's the point in staying together?'

He pushed me. 'Go to hell.'

We didn't speak to each other for the next two days. But otherwise, life went on normally.

After two days, I found an envelope kept on the table— on the same table where he had mentioned once that he had purposefully kept his Paris tickets for me to see. I thought it might be a sorry card or a letter.

It's normal to have a fight as husband and wife. Once upon a time, I used to complain that he didn't fight with me. Rather, he preferred to leave the house. You see, he had changed now. He cared for me and he needed me. That's why he was concerned.

I opened the envelope and took out the papers. It was not handwritten but printed sheets. It read:

The Divorce Act, 1869
Dissolution of marriage, mutual consent, nullity
of marriage, judicial separation, and restitution of
conjugal right under the Indian Divorce Act, 1869.

Chapter 24

Respect Yourself

Till now, it was just a game of hide-and-seek.

I was crystal clear about my goals and my destination. If I had asked, dreamt, and prayed anything in love, that was only from Raghav. Neel came into my life from nowhere. But did my attitude change for Raghav just because I knew that there was someone who would always be there to hold my hand? Did I think more and care more for Neel now? I think I did, but what's wrong in that? He understood me much more than Raghav had ever tried to.

I wanted to talk to Neel. I sent him a message, 'Want to meet you. Need to talk to you urgently.'

Five minutes later, a message flashed on my mobile screen. 'In a meeting now. Meet me 5 p.m. sharp at McDonald's near your house.'

There were still two hours. I booked my air tickets for Mumbai–Delhi, then rail tickets from Delhi to Kathgodam, the last railway station to reach Almora. There was no need to pre-book from Kathgodam to Almora, as you could get a taxi every fifteen minutes.

Five sharp, I reached McDonald's, which was hardly ten minutes' walk from my place. Neel was already there, waiting outside in formals, as he had come straight from the meeting. There was a tinge of tiredness on his face, but his caring attitude was shining bright. On seeing me, he walked towards me. 'What happened? Hope everything is fine.'

We went upstairs and sat on a corner table without ordering anything.

'Not actually.' I tried to smile, but it was fully soaked in artificiality.

'I know something is grossly wrong. You can trust me, Riya.'

With eyes full of tears, I narrated to him everything—what had happened while coming back from Sahil's party and in the night following that.

'Okay, now first stop crying like a baby. We will find a solution.' He took some tissue paper from the stand and offered it to me. He ordered coffee and burger.

I tried to control it a bit. 'Neel, I will ask you one thing.'
'Yes. Please.'

'I always loved Raghav, tried to keep him happy, never complained for five years—then you came into my life, but I always remembered my limits—to the extent that I am even tolerating Sara. Now what else does he expect from me? I don't know what's so bad in me.'

'Riya, I will tell you one thing—you are a nice girl. Rather, the nicest girl I have ever met in my life. All of us have our positives and negatives. You see, you can be the ripest, juiciest peach in the world, but still, there are people who hate peaches. That's not your fault.'

I smiled.

'Have you thought of one thing, Riya? Suppose I am just saying that if things get even worse tomorrow. Do you have a plan B in your mind?'

'What do you mean?'

'I don't know how to put it, but in case something happens—things between you two start getting more complicated or Raghav decides to be with Sara—have you thought what you are going to do?'

'No. Neel, I was not forced into this marriage. I married Raghav because I liked him. I fell in love with him. Now after so many years, I realize I don't love him anymore. What does it mean? Today I may feel I love someone else. What is the guarantee that tomorrow things will remain the same?'

'What I feel is that everybody is not made for everybody. We can't be compatible or happy with everyone in this world. Because we made a wrong decision in life for whatever reason, we are not bound to curse ourselves in our whole lifetime for that.'

I was getting confused on what he wanted to say.

'No hurry. Think about it sometime.'

He paused for a while and looked at his mobile. 'Oh yeah, I will tell you some good news—Mom and Dad are coming.'

'When?'

'Tickets are not yet confirmed, but towards the month end. I will take you home then, and I promise that nothing like the last time will happen.' He winked.

'But I am going home on the 26th. I want to stay with Mom and Dad for a month or so. That place refreshes me. I am tired, really tired, Neel.'

'I understand. But what about your treatment? You told me the other day that your report has come and you will have to get admitted in the hospital again for something.'

'Yeah, but the doctor told me that one or two months don't matter. I can take my time to decide.'

'Decide? Decide what?'

'Same thing, whether I want to have just the cone removal and then follow-ups or removal of the uterus itself.'

'What's there to decide, Riya?'

'Means?'

'Obviously, it is not removal of the uterus. I thought you just said that to hurt Raghav's ego and feel better.'

'No. I am serious.'

'Don't be lunatic. Think for a while.'

'Why? When your mom had to get her breast removed, did you also say the same thing?'

Neel tried to calm down. 'Listen to me carefully now. When Mom got her problem, she was already fifty-three, and you are not even thirty, Riya. Mom had a frank cancer, with no other option. You said you only have a pre-cancer, which can be managed with conservative surgery.'

'I have made my decision. You may call me fussy, adamant, or rude—whatever you want to.'

'Look, Riya. Just look at the other side. Your relationship with Raghav already is under a lot of stress because of Sara. Now he has got some divorce papers also, according to you. Suppose something happens tomorrow and you two decide to separate . . .'

'Yes, I am ready for that. Do you think I care now? I am anyways going to sign those papers the day I leave for Almora. I'll let him keep on filling the details whenever he wants to.'

'Will you let me finish?'

'Yeah, please.'

'So if you, tomorrow, after your separation, decide to start your new life again . . .'

'What?'

'Do you still want to get your uterus removed? Think about it,' he said in a single breath.

'Now you tell me, Neel Agarwal, my turn to ask you something, if that girl you told me about the other day, God forbid, required something like this, will this change your feeling for her?'

He looked straight at me for a while. I waited for his answer, staring blankly at him.

He didn't say anything. He called the waiter and asked, 'Can I have the check, please.'

In his hesitation, I found my answer. I told him bye and walked away—more free, more confident.

Sometimes walking away is the only option—not because you want to make someone miss you or realize they took you for granted but because you finally start respecting yourself enough to know that you deserve better. You are better alone.

Chapter 25

Almora Again

O n these convoluted roads between the green
mountains on the way from Kathgodam to Almora,
a thought clicked my mind, *A bend in the road is not the
end of the road unless you fail to make the right turn at
the right time.*

After our last meeting at McDonald's, which had not
ended at an ecstatic note as it used to be, Neel tried calling
me many times, but I didn't receive his call. There was
nothing to talk about. I didn't want his opinion any more.

I landed up in Delhi sometime in the afternoon, and
then my train Ranikhet Express started around eleven thirty
after a delay of around thirty minutes. In the morning when
I got up, we were approaching Kathgodam. My watch
showed 5 a.m., and it was bright outside. I stood near the
door. Cold breeze touched my cheeks, my hair, and my soul.
It was blissful. It had been three years since I had been to
this route. I remembered the last time. Raghav was with me,
and we stood here together hand in hand.

I thought about Raghav, what he could be doing, what
he could be thinking. But I couldn't imagine anything
other than the snapshot of the divorce papers and Sara in
succession. For a second, Neel's face came in front of me,

but by the time, with a shriek of whistle, the train had slowly come to a standstill. I took my luggage and went towards the taxi stand. I wanted to have coffee after booking the taxi, though the driver suggested that we could have breakfast at Bhimtal, which was just forty-five minutes away. I agreed.

'How much time will it take to reach Almora?' I asked.

'It is eighty kilometres, but roads are not good, so it will take four hours.' Bhola, the driver, who was basically from a village near Almora, asked, 'Madam, first time to Almora?'

'Do you think so? I was born and brought up here.'

'Oh, good, good,' he said.

We kept on chatting for some time about his family and his life, which he very enthusiastically shared with me.

When I told him that I live in Mumbai, Bhola was excited to the core. He confessed that his dream is to become a Bollywood star one day like Salman Khan. I smiled. *Bhola* means 'innocent'. I hoped life had been so simple, so innocent, without any prejudice for dreams and realities.

We reached Bhimtal. Bhimtal is a picturesque lake centred amidst foliate mountains. This view had always fascinated me whenever I crossed this area. This lake derived its name from the legendry Bheema in *Mahabharata*, Dad had told me a long time ago. This lake is a scenic spot with a small island in its centre where you can go by a boat. It had a restaurant, I remember. I asked Bhola, 'Bhola, can we go to the island to have breakfast if you are not in a hurry?'

'Madam, I am not in a hurry, but the restaurant is closed. Instead, the government had made an aquarium there. We can go and see that.'

'No, I am not interested in seeing an aquarium now.'

So we went to a simple small restaurant at the corner where Bhola had parked his taxi. I took tea and onion *pakora.* I offered him to sit with me, but Bhola denied and stood outside the restaurant with his tea and plate of *pakora.*

We started again in twenty to twenty-five minutes.

Though I started getting motion sickness on these curvy roads, I didn't want to close my eyes, for I didn't want to miss to capture any scenery on the way. The hills looked beautiful in October. Tiny yellow and white flowers in the lush green palisades were making it more titillating. On the way, it drizzled a bit. The feeling of tiny droplets touching my palm had a healing effect. It washed away all my tiredness, anxiety, soreness, and negativity. I felt rejuvenated, reborn.

That's why I feel people used to come here and become saints. The air from the hills has this magic. The beauty of these hills has captivated millions, including Swami Vivekananda, who meditated in the pristine air of Almora. Jawaharlal Nehru, during the British rule, served a term of imprisonment in the jail at Almora. He mentioned the elaborate account of the pleasures of solitude and the varied moods of nature in his letters written from jail to his daughter. Rabindranath Tagore spent a summer to get over his personal grief after the loss of his wife and daughter. And now I was here to test the healing magic of these hills. I was anxious, I was troubled, I was distressed, and you were my only hope. I planned to stay with Mom and Dad for a week then join the famous yoga and meditation centre there. I had come here in search of peace . . . peace for my shattered soul.

———— ✦ ————

I ate, I slept, I gossiped. It was my home. I was happy. I felt as if I were Miss Riya Suri again. I went to the nearby areas with Dad, but I realized that it was not the same as how I left it. Now there were unplanned constructions everywhere, with no proper thought about the waste disposal. The temples still had the serenity, but the maintenance was lacking. The markets were overcrowded, with shops eating up half of the walking area. After a few days, I preferred staying home and watching the mountains from the rooftop.

One morning, I felt like opening Facebook. Having come here, I had decided not to touch the Internet. But somehow today, I wanted to break my promises to myself and get the headlines of Facebook. I thought maybe Neel had posted some pics with his mom and dad, as they must also have reached Mumbai last week.

Life was as usual in it—friends were posing, advertising their affections, reviewing movies and songs, and sharing jokes. Not interested in all the same happenings in the world, I went straight to Neel's page and felt thunderstruck. His relationship status had changed from 'single' to 'in a relationship', and his latest post read, 'Going to propose to her. Wish me luck.'

I knew it has to happen very soon. *His mom and dad must also have agreed*, I thought, but all this was causing some sort of cramp inside me. Without thinking much, I deleted my Facebook account and shut down the laptop.

Buddha rightly said, 'The root of suffering is attachment.' No attachment, no suffering.

Chapter 26

Peace Redefined

Nothing binds you except your thoughts.
Nothing limits you except your fears.
Nothing controls you except your beliefs.

I read this, written at the main entrance of the yoga and meditation centre.

I went straight inside to the reception and showed them the printed copy of my registration for the three-week course. It was supposed to start tomorrow morning, so I decided to check in today.

While the lady in a white sari was busy penning down my details, I asked her, 'How many participants do you allow in a batch?'

She replied in a soft and serene voice, 'Usually ten, but till today, in this batch, we have only eight registrations.'

I waited for a moment and then reemphasized my preference, 'And I had requested for a single room.'

'Yes, miss. I am checking availability of the same.' She smiled.

'Take your time.'

'Miss, we had kept room number 7 for you, but Mr Davidson wants to continue his course for two more weeks, and he is not ready to shift to room number 13. He is requesting us to retain the same room for him, so if you don't mind, number 13.'

'In simple words, you only have one single room left, which is number 13.'

'Yes, miss,' she hesitated.

'No probs. I shall take it happily.'

She gave me a big smile and handed over the key. I took my bag and reached my room without any problem. On the other side of the reception area, there was a small garden which had two boards on its two ends. One read 'Single Room and Meditation Hall', and the other read 'Double Rooms and Yoga Arena'. I took the first road, and on the fourth block, my room was on the upper storey. Every block had four rooms—first two on the first floor and the next two on the ground floor.

After climbing around ten stairs, I unlocked the door of room number 13. It was a small room with mere basic amenities. I kept my bag on the table, opened the other door, which opened straight into the combined balcony with room number 14. The view was so serene. We were at the summit of the hill. I could see the whole valley from there. Just a few hundred metres away was the river which always fascinated me during my childhood days, and when my eyes turned to my left, I found that small white temple so close to me. I was relaxed. I looked forward to my stay here.

On the next day, as per the instructions, I got up at 4 a.m. sharp, took a cold-water shower, changed the pure-white kurta pyjamas provided to me, pulled back my hair together to tie it into a high ponytail, looked at my fragrance hesitatingly, and sprayed it a little.

At 4.45 a.m., I was waiting for the guruji with five other members of the group at the meditation hall. Some of them were chatting with each other, but most of them were silent. I also had decided that my motive for coming here was to find peace and to rediscover and know my own self. I was not interested in friends and friendship here.

At 5 a.m. sharp, the guruji entered. Following him were two other guys. I thought the guruji also had got his assistants with him, but no, I was wrong. They were two members who had also registered for the same course.

The guruji sat on a posture called *sukhasana* and instructed us also to assume the same position. He explained, 'In Sanskrit, *sukh* means "ease", "happiness", "peace", or "relaxation", and this pose is aimed at providing all of it.' Following that, he told us to close our eyes for two minutes and try not to think about anything.

When all of us opened our eyes in more or less two minutes, he started in his deep voice, 'Meditation is not just relaxation. Its primary purpose is to develop the capacity to respond gracefully to the difficulties of life as well as the joys of life.'

The atmosphere was serene. The gentle breeze blowing through the large open windows was refreshing. Birds had started chirping in the jungle to welcome the rising sun.

The guruji's words in his husky deep voice were music to the ears. He said, 'Meditation and yoga are like the two hemispheres of our brain: the right and the left. Complimentary to each other. *Yoga* is a Sanskrit word that means "to add", "to join", "to unite", or "to attach". It is a practice to unite with your own self. Uniting with your own self imparts discipline to your existence. It's a unifying experience for your body and mind. On the other hand, mediation is the process to unite your mind with your soul. The word *meditation* has been derived from the Latin word *meditatio* or *meditari*, which means "to think", "to contemplate", or "to ponder".'

He paused for a minute, looked at us, and continued, 'I agree that it is not easy to understand and implement what I am saying—to unite your body with your mind and then your mind with your soul. But that's what you have come here for, and in the coming twenty-one days, it is my responsibility to make you understand what I am saying, not through talking and lecturing but through practice and implementation.'

'So now, we will sit in silence for twenty minutes at a stretch, and then we will go to the riverside, where in front of the rising sun, I will teach you *surya namaskar*.'

The nine of us reached the riverbank barefoot. As per the instruction, eight of us stood behind the guruji in a horizontal row, facing the rising sun. He told us to follow him. We performed a set of twelve different asanas with him. 'This is called one set of surya namaskar, or "salutation to the sun". If you are pressed for time and looking for a single mantra to stay fit, this is the answer.'

'Oh really?' One of the students wondered.

'Yes, this asana is a set of twelve powerful yoga postures that provide a good cardiovascular workout to keep the body in shape and the mind calm and healthy.'

'First of all, follow me on this: "O Lord Surya! O sun of suns, the eye of the world, the eye of the *virat-purusha*, thou art all energy, all strength, all-powerful. Please give me health, strength, vigour, and vitality."'

With folded hands and closed eyes, we repeated with him, the same thing, in Sanskrit.

And then we repeated all the asanas of surya namaskar till we were exhausted as per our capacity and stamina. *Shavasana* (posture of dead) felt amazingly relaxing after this.

'Now I am leaving you all with yourself,' the guruji said.

You may have yogic breakfast in the kitchen, then you are free to do whatever you like. I suggest you to indulge in one of your hobbies which you don't get time to perform in the hustle of your routine life. It can be painting, writing, sketching, singing, reading, or dancing in rhythm . . . anything you feel like doing for yourself.'

The idea sounded interesting.

'We shall meet again at seven in the prayer room.' And he left.

Day after day, it followed the same way. Thoughts started becoming more and more transparent, tranquilized, enlightening, and fulfilling.

It was the sixteenth day of the course. In the morning, during the surya namaskar, we were performing *parvatasana*, which means mountain posture. I was on all fours like an animal with buttocks lifted off and limbs stretched, which simulated like a mountain. A figure came in front of my eyes, though upside down. I stopped and stood erect. I kept both my palms over my closed eyes and felt disgusted. *Why can't I forget him for God's sake?*

I went to the side, drank some water from my bottle, and started again with more concentration and energy.

While we were going back, Pooja, the gardener's seven-year-old daughter, shouted from the garden area in front of the reception, 'Riya didi, there is someone who wants to meet you. Some uncle.'

Her words changed the direction of my footsteps towards the reception. I felt irritated. *Dad, please, I am grown-up now. Stop following me as if I were a little girl*, I thought inside.

The guruji's words echoed within, *Calm down, calm down.* I stopped. *You can't calm the storm. So stop trying. What you can do is calm yourself. The storm will pass.* When I thought about this, I smiled brightly and moved. *Dad is not less than a storm.*

My smile was not yet over, and I was at the entrance to the reception. Two men were sitting on the wooden bench. The more visible one had a spiritual magazine in front of his face, more or less hiding his face. The younger one was bent on himself in such a way that his face was facing the ground and a tuft of curly hair was gazing me. My smile evaporated and transformed into a question mark.

It was a mistake, I realized. None of them was Dad.

I screamed, 'Pooja, Are you sure the call was for me?'

I am not sure whether Pooja heard it or not, but the two men did. The younger one stood up. I recognized the face on the other side of the curly tuft. 'Neel.'

What now? Why is he here? I thought.

He smiled from the distance.

A voice echoed again, *Calm down. This storm shall also pass.*

I started walking towards him. A thought glimpsed inside, *Oh, he has come to invite me now. So far. He has managed to search me to give the invitation card. Yes, why not? I am his best friend, indeed.* Bitterness was spilling out despite my efforts to control it.

I don't know whether it is right or wrong, but they say hatred is not the opposite of love. It's love gone wrong somewhere. Opposite of love is called apathy.

I reached near him. He greeted softly, 'Hi. How are you?'

Bluntly I said, 'Where is the card? I don't accept oral invites.'

He stared at me without blinking even once. 'There is still time, I guess. The girl has not officially said yes.'

'Is she stupid or you?' my analytical self blurted out.

Next moment, he was in front of me on his knees. On his left palm was a tiny box with a glitter inside. 'The next moment shall decide.'

There was silence—pindrop silence. The moment froze as did I. I could feel the warmth of tears rolling down on my cheeks.

The silence broke. 'The moment is waiting to know . . . who is stupid? The girl or me?'

I couldn't say anything. Covering my face with both my palms, I smiled and cried at the same time. With the sound of Pooja's tiny hands clapping slowly, I regained consciousness of the time, place, and person. I looked around. The elder man, the registration girls, Shambhu, and Pooja—all were standing there, smiling, smiling from within.

I blushed, blushed red. I pulled Neel's hand, and he followed towards the exit. We didn't speak a word, but our hands were held tight. We dipped our feet in the river and sat on the edge under the shade of a tree. I placed my head on his shoulder. He wrapped his arm tightly around me. 'Riya, I want to confess something. The first day I said I was falling in love with you, I was not flirting. It was as if somehow I was destined to meet you. There was a feeling very strange, very deep.' I was enjoying his words, his voice, the feeling within . . . everything. He continued with his eyes towards the skyline as if he were living in the same time zone of those initial days when we had started chatting. 'I had gone crazy about you. I had decided that I will have either you or no one.'

'Then from where did that girl come? Your old friend?'

He looked at me, smiling. 'Silly girl, I was talking about you, but I didn't want to admit anything before I told my mom and dad about it.' He paused, 'The day you told me about the divorce papers thing, please forgive me for that, but I was the happiest soul on this earth.'

It was my turn to smile. 'I wanted you to meet Mom and Dad, but you were so adamant about your programme. Having discussed it with my parents, I didn't waste a moment. I did not even apply leave in the office. My FB status was self-explanatory.'

And what were you imagining, Riya? my heart asked me. I ducked inside his embrace.

Remembering something, I said hesitantly, 'But I can't give you a baby.'

He was ready with an answer to this. 'No issues. I have done enough research.' He took out a small cutting of paper from his wallet. 'If you are not comfortable with surrogacy, I will meet this Professor Barnstorm and ask him to implant a uterus on me.'

I giggled. He kissed my forehead, saying, 'Anything for your smile.'

And it was the most luscious moment of my entire lifetime. I understood. No alcohol, no meditation, and no yoga can offer this unified and amalgamated peace of body, heart, mind, and soul as a kiss of heartfelt love can.

This is the truth! The eternal truth!

Epilogue

It has been thirteen years (exactly thirteen) since I have come back from my first foreign exposure or Europe experience—or in other words, after the most volcanic year of my life, mentally, mystically, and medically.

At the moment, I am very close to the same white temple I used to see from my window when I was a child. We are having a relaxed dinner at the rooftop of a la-di-da resort—Neel, Diya, and I. It looks heavenly from this point, as if we were hanging inside a sphere of stars—the twinkling starts above and the many thousand lights spread in the town, producing an illusion of static stars, below.

I am in Almora. No, not for a vacation but for the inauguration of our fifth resort in the chain called Neelriya Rejuvenation Resorts (NRR group). It all started in 2014 with the first resort in the Swiss Alps. Neel left his job at Oracle to start his dream venture. It was a complete Indian-style resort dedicated to rejuvenation with meditation, yoga, and Indian food (purely vegetarian), meant for those who seek solace in either the monotony and platitude or turbulence and chaos of life.

After the colossal success and welcome of this concept, we opened the second one in Greece, and the third in Maldives. This one was the second in India after a successful and accomplishing experiment in Lavasa a year ago. Opening a resort here was the most precious adventure for us. Exactly thirteen years ago at the same place, we decided to start our life together.

One of the main areas of focus of the newer governments was to promote tourism. People involved in tourism investment were being promoted as never before. Every minister was instructed to adopt at least one tourist destination and develop it.

As a result, Almora too was transformed. From a place of mushrooming haphazard construction, spoiled roads, and dirty, clumsy, and overcrowded markets, now Almora had a neat and breathtaking picture. It had direct connectivity with Dehradun and Pantnagar airports, with its seducing serpentine roads. There was a chopper service too, which was active only during summer season though.

The town, situated in a crescent-shaped mountain ridge, not more than five kilometres long, bordered by two rivers (Kosi and Suyal), now is divided into seven zones from north to south. Each zone is given a colour from the rainbow (VIBGYOR) in a sequence. A particular zone has the name of the colour, and the whole infrastructure of that zone is painted in the same colour. Pictures shot here from the helicopters are one of the most-admired pictures in the global tourist destination sites. The rising sun from somewhere behind the lush green hills, the flowing streak of river, and the semicircle of rainbow patches looked nothing less than a land of fairies.

We bought ten acres of land on this hilltop surrounding the temple, which also included the yoga and meditation centre that changed my life forever in every sense. Destroying it was out of question. We upgraded it, gave it a modern look with all the possible facilities, and built a row of captivating log huts parallel to the river, with all the amenities to experience traditional yogic life. We kept everything in the property pure white, keeping in mind that there were already too many colours in the town.

What about me? I was not working full-time anywhere. I helped Neel in his dream projects. CCA had patented a panel of nine genes for triage of HPV-positive cases in the future. They were working with those genes in population-based samples from all around the world in a multi-centric adventure, which involved ten centres across the globe.

I got invitations to deliver lectures for short-term project or to scrutinize results among those centres. And whenever I got some time, I spent it in writing. It's easy to calculate how busy life keeps me—just with the fact that it took me thirteen long years to pen down my own story!

After our divorce, Raghav started staying with Sara in the same apartment in Mumbai. I forgot and forgave, as I realized Raghav didn't do anything intentionally. It was forced on him by our conservative social norms and mindset. I had no bitter feelings, no negativity in life.

Meanwhile, I gave birth to a princess after a stormy pregnancy. I conceived during the third cycle of IVF. They put a stitch in my cervix in the fourth month to keep it tight, as I had undergone a minor surgery on my cervix (conization) earlier for which Neel had managed to convince me. I went into preterm labour at thirty-four weeks, and we were blessed with Diya on 13 August. She was kept in NICU for a month, but she is a strong girl, now three years old. Her third birthday we celebrated with the inauguration of the resort. Diya is the light that brightens our days.

'Mommy, from that mountain had your Prince Charming come riding his horse?' she asked.

'Yeah, I guess.'

Neel interrupted, 'Mommy has got confused. I came from that one, from where the sun rises.' And we laughed.

She thought for a while and asked, 'Then from where will my prince come? I am just wondering.'

Neel threw his arm around my waist, pulled me closer and winked. 'Your genes are getting expressed, Riya Madam.'

Appendix

The Factual HPV and Cervical Cancer Story

C ervix, which is the lower part of the uterus (or the womb), can have a deadly cancer. This cancer of the cervix is the fourth most common cancer in women, with an estimated 500,000 new cases occurring worldwide every year. This cancer leads to around 250,000 deaths per year.

Though cervical cancer occurs around or after forty years of age, the story starts much earlier. As soon as a girl becomes sexually active, she has a risk of getting infected with HPV virus. HPV infection now has been proven to be the most important risk factor for cervical cancer. This HPV virus usually gets eliminated from our body because of our immune system, but in some cases, it persists and gives rise to a series of events at cellular level. Scientifically, these changes are known as low-grade and high-grade lesions. Both low- and high-grade lesions together are also known as pre-cancer or pre-malignant lesions. Usually, low-grade lesions are self-limiting but can progress to a high-grade lesion. High-grade lesion usually develops into frank cancer. This HPV to cervical cancer progression takes around ten years.

Cervical cancer is among the very few cancers which have been understood well and can be prevented. The first thing which we can do to protect ourselves is vaccination with HPV vaccine. This vaccine is available in the market and is given to young girls at around twelve to thirteen years of age or before their sexual debut. This vaccine prevents us from around 70 per cent of deadly (high-risk) HPV virus which can cause the cancer. But this vaccine alone is not enough for total prevention. *Using condoms* helps to prevent transmission of virus from one partner to another. Likewise, it's understandable that monogamous relationship (that means both partners having only one partner) also reduces this risk. To provide further protection, detection at pre-cancer stage is the second thing. The pre-cancer stage is 100 per cent curable. It has been recommended that women should routinely undergo Pap smear test (with or without HPV test). In Pap test, a doctor scrapes some cells from the woman's cervix, makes a slide, and sends this to be studied under a microscope. This microscopic study helps to tell if there are abnormal cells (low grade lesions, high grade lesions, or cancer cells). Now, if the report comes as one of these, usually the doctor asks the patient to get a test known as colposcopy. Colposcopy gives a magnified view of the cervix with a magnifying machine called colposcope. With the help of this machine, biopsies can be taken from abnormal areas. If the report of the biopsy reveals low grade lesions, the patient just requires follow-up with Pap smears. If the report reveals high grade lesions, this requires removal of a complete cone of tissue from the cervix, where usually the cancer develops. After the conization procedure, the patient also has to be followed up with Pap smear. If the Pap smear or biopsy taken from the cervix shows a frank cancer, much more extensive treatment is required. Once there is cancer, it becomes a little problematic situation. However, if detected in early stages and treated adequately, it also carries a fair prognosis.

Late stages of cervical cancer are deadly and associated with high mortality and complications. In the era when we know everything about cervical cancer and its prevention, a lady dying because of it is genuinely an unfortunate event.

Defeat Cervical Cancer: 3D
Decide Vaccination
Defy Unsafe Sex
Demand Screening

Brief Synopsis

Riya, the girl next door, is very much one among us. Being born in a simple middle-class family in a small town of India and growing up with big dreams and aspiration, she doesn't know that the real name of life is 'compromise' and 'settle down with what you get easily'. And then she gets a ravishing opportunity interregnum she falls in love, a virtual one though. Life starts changing its colours.

Life is going fine, but a test done just for curiosity changes everything. She is broken mentally and emotionally. What is her fault for which she is being punished? Does love really exist? Or is the expression of love also just a matter of convenience?

The focus of this book is to create awareness about HPV and cervical cancer prevention among the young generation. It talks about vaccination, safe sexual practices, screening, and consequences, which I feel every boy and girl in the society should know. Cervical cancer is unique, as it is completely preventable and the changes start much early in life (in the age group of twenties to thirties), progressing to cancer later in life. This is the tender age mostly when health issues are not in the priority list. The idea is to present the information in the form of a romantic fiction so that the message remains interesting, readable, and better retained.

Author Biography

Dr Deeksha Pandey born and brought up in Almora, graduated from King Georges Medical College (KGMC), Lucknow, is presently a consultant gynaecologist and associate professor (OBG) in one of the top-notch medical schools in India (Kasturba Medical College, Manipal).

Eradication of cervical cancer is her passion. For the last ten years, she has been involved in treating, teaching, creating awareness, and discovering new markers so as to control the disease and its consequences. She has got many international fellowships and travel awards to Amsterdam, Australia, Canada, Chicago, Germany, Hong Kong and Taiwan to work and learn in the dominion and has published many scientific papers. This is her effort for the society to learn how to take care of themselves from this easily acquired, deadly disease which is 100 per cent preventable.

She currently resides in Manipal with her husband, Dr Vivek Pandey (orthopaedic surgeon), and son Krish.

Defeat Cervical Cancer: **3D**
Decide Vaccination
Defy Unsafe Sex
Demand Screening